"I adore children,"

Danielle said cheerfully. "Your boys will be just fine with me, Slade."

"They're something of a handful," Slade observed.

Talk about an understatement! Yet the handsome widower sounded so weary that Dani immediately wanted to throw her arms around him and tell him everything would be all right.

This was the role she was born to play: mother, wife, nurturer. And never had she seen a family so in need of what she had to offer.

Suddenly, as that thought registered, an outrageous idea began to blossom. Perhaps Slade Watkins and his two sons were the opportunity she'd been waiting for. Perhaps her dream was finally within her grasp.

But how could she convince Slade she was the answer to *his* prayers?

Well, first things first. His boys needed a mother, no doubt about that.

The question remaining was when Slade would realize…he needed a wife!

Dear Reader,

April is the time for the little things...a time for nature to nurture new growth, a time for spring to begin to show its glory.

So, it's perfect timing to have a THAT'S MY BABY! title this month. *What To Do About Baby* by award-winning author Martha Hix is a tender, humorous tale about a heroine who discovers love in the most surprising ways. After her estranged mother's death, the last thing Caroline Grant expected to inherit was an eighteen-month-old sister...or to fall in love with the handsome stranger who delivered the surprise bundle!

And more springtime fun is in store for our readers as Sherryl Woods's wonderful series THE BRIDAL PATH continues with the delightful *Danielle's Daddy Factor*. Next up, Pamela Toth's BUCKLES & BRONCOS series brings you back to the world of the beloved Buchanan brothers when their long-lost sister, Kirby, is found—and is about to discover romance in *Buchanan's Return*.

What is spring without a wedding? *Stop the Wedding!* by Trisha Alexander is sure to win your heart! And don't miss Janis Reams Hudson's captivating story of reunited lovers in *The Mother of His Son*. And a surefire keeper is coming your way in *A Stranger to Love* by Patricia McLinn. This tender story promises to melt your heart!

I hope you enjoy each and every story this month!

Sincerely,

Tara Gavin,
Senior Editor

Please address questions and book requests to:
Silhouette Reader Service
U.S.: 3010 Walden Ave., P.O. Box 1325, Buffalo, NY 14269
Canadian: P.O. Box 609, Fort Erie, Ont. L2A 5X3

SHERRYL WOODS
DANIELLE'S DADDY FACTOR

Published by Silhouette Books
America's Publisher of Contemporary Romance

SILHOUETTE BOOKS

ISBN 0-373-24094-5

DANIELLE'S DADDY FACTOR

Books by Sherryl Woods

Silhouette Special Edition

Safe Harbor #425
Never Let Go #446
Edge of Forever #484
In Too Deep #522
Miss Liz's Passion #573
Tea and Destiny #595
My Dearest Cal #669
Joshua and the Cowgirl #713
*Love #769
*Honor #775
*Cherish #781
*Kate's Vow #823
*A Daring Vow #855
*A Vow To Love #885
The Parson's Waiting #907
One Step Away #927
Riley's Sleeping Beauty #961
†Finally a Bride #987
‡A Christmas Blessing #1001
‡Natural Born Daddy #1007
‡The Cowboy and His Baby #1009
‡The Rancher and
  His Unexpected Daughter #1016
**A Ranch for Sara #1083
**Ashley's Rebel #1087
**Danielle's Daddy Factor #1094

Silhouette Desire

Not at Eight, Darling #309
Yesterday's Love #329
Come Fly with Me #345
A Gift of Love #375
Can't Say No #431
Heartland #472
One Touch of Moondust #521
Next Time...Forever #601
Fever Pitch #620
Dream Mender #708

Silhouette Books

Silhouette Summer Sizzlers 1990
"A Bridge to Dreams"

*Vows
†Always a Bridesmaid!
‡And Baby Makes Three
**The Bridal Path

SHERRYL WOODS

lives by the ocean, which, she says, provides daily inspiration for the romance in her soul. She further explains that her years as a television critic taught her about steamy plots and humor; her years as a travel editor took her to exotic locations; and her years as a crummy weekend tennis player taught her to stick with what she enjoyed most—writing. "What better way is there," Sherryl asks, "to combine all that experience than by creating romantic stories?" Sherryl loves to hear from her readers. You may write to her at P.O. Box 490326, Key Biscayne, FL 33149. A self-addressed, stamped envelope is appreciated for a reply.

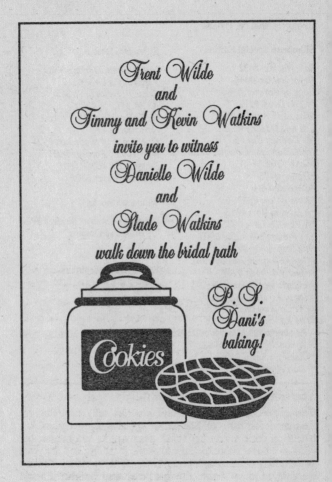

Trent Wilde
and
Timmy and Kevin Watkins
invite you to witness
Danielle Wilde
and
Slade Watkins
walk down the bridal path

P. S.
Dani's
baking!

Cookies

Chapter One

Danielle Wilde was pushing thirty, unmarried and mad as hell about it. The oldest of rancher Trent Wilde's three daughters, she'd planned to be a mother several times over by now. She'd set the goal the first time she'd cradled a doll in her arms, and never once had she wavered from it. Okay, once. The first time she'd held her squalling baby sister, she might have had a few doubts. She'd been little more than a baby herself at the time, so that hardly counted.

At any rate, in a goal-oriented family like hers, she was pretty much a failure. Strong-willed Sara was operating the family ranch, just as she'd always envisioned. Ashley, the prettiest and brightest, had had a spectacular run as a successful cover model before settling down again back home in Riverton.

And here she was, living like a spinster in a small house in town, successfully selling her jams and baked goods to the general store and playing the piano in church on Sundays. Her life was so tame and predictable, so completely and thoroughly single, it made her want to spit.

Seeing both of her younger sisters marry the men of their dreams this past year hadn't helped a bit, either. Sara had quite literally bet the ranch on the outcome of a bronco ride to win ex-rodeo champ Jake Dawson. Ashley had bopped reformed rebel Dillon Ford on the head with a lamp, then turned that inauspicious reunion into a fiery, devil-may-care romance that had set the whole town on its ear. Both sisters were blissfully happy.

She was thrilled for them, she really was, but oh, how she longed for the same thing for herself. Dani sighed just thinking about the grit and determination her sisters had employed to get the men and the life-styles they wanted. Nothing had stood in their way, least of all their meddling father, who had his own ideas about the choices they should make for their lives. Sara and Ashley were masters of their own destinies, willing to do the most outrageous things if that's what it took to get what they wanted.

The most outrageous thing she had ever done was spill a little flour on the kitchen floor and leave it there overnight.

As for men, the only ones in town worth having were already taken or were so old that the mere thought of children underfoot gave them heart palpitations.

Her meddling father had picked out a couple of the latter for her, and if she couldn't come up with an alternative fast, his suggestions were likely to start making sense. The very thought of marrying for little more than companionship had her pounding her latest batch of bread dough so fiercely the loaves were likely to be the consistency of bricks.

Sucking in a deep, calming breath, she stared at the flat mess she'd created and choked back a cry of despair—not over the bread so much as her whole pitiful, dull existence.

"Well, drat," she muttered and threw the entire batch of dough into the trash before starting over from scratch to make the round, crusty, country bread that sold so well to locals and tourists.

If only it were so easy to set her life onto a new, more exciting course, she thought as she sifted flour into a huge bowl. Her hand stilled as she heard a muffled exchange on her back porch, followed by what just might have been childish laughter and the distinct, frenzied barking of a dog.

Intrigued, she was halfway to the window to peek out when a loud crash and the clanging sound of metal against wood set off a stampede of scurrying footsteps, her own among them. She had the back door open in a split second. The sight that greeted her would have reduced a lesser woman to tears.

Her pies, her beautiful blueberry pies, were upended all over the porch. All except for one, that is.

In the hands of a towheaded boy of ten or so, it was being mashed into the face of what appeared to be his similarly towheaded younger brother.

Meanwhile, the ugliest mongrel dog she had ever seen—a mix of black and brown and white patches—was racing around the two of them in circles, barking in a raspy way that sounded as if it had laryngitis. The dog was catching clumps of spilling blueberries with great glee.

"I told you you were going to make a mess of it," the older boy was saying, apparently oblivious to his own obvious contribution to the very visible disaster. "I told you. Just look what you've done."

The younger one's response was cut off by another mouthful of pie being stuffed in his face.

Dani cleared her throat loudly. Two matching pairs of blue eyes, wide as saucers, jerked her way. Both boys froze, creating a tableau of blueberry-covered, childish dismay. The dog, alerted that something had shifted, skidded to a halt in front of Dani, tail wagging, head cocked, blueberry stains all over his graying muzzle.

"Ohmigosh," the littlest boy muttered, wiping sticky streaks from his face with the tail end of his shirt, quickly turning it into a laundry nightmare. "Dad's going to kill us."

"Deader than a doornail," the older one agreed solemnly. With his gaze fixed hopefully on Dani, he pleaded, "Could you, maybe, not tell him? We'd make it up to you somehow. We promise. Please?"

Faced with such a winsome appeal despite their

blatant guilt, Dani couldn't decide whether to laugh or cry. Forcing herself to take the expected stern tone, she said, "Perhaps you'd better explain just what happened here before I make any decisions."

"It was his idea," the littlest boy said, earning a disgusted look from his brother for the betrayal. "Timmy is always getting us into trouble."

"Do not," Timmy declared. "It's you, Kevin. If you weren't such a screwup, we never would have gotten caught."

"You said nobody was home," Kevin countered.

"That didn't mean you could knock everything over. We were just supposed to steal one." Timmy turned to Dani and rolled his eyes. "He's only eight and he's really pretty uncoordinated for a boy. This kind of stuff happens all the time."

"Does it really?" Dani asked dryly, staring at the mess on her porch. "This bad?"

"Worse sometimes," Timmy vowed. "Dad yells at us all the time."

"All the time," Kevin concurred, nodding solemnly.

"He says we're going to be the death of him yet," Timmy added.

"Or wind up in juvenile hall," Kevin said, his voice suddenly quivering and his eyes filling with tears. "Please don't send us to jail." The dog, sensing some sort of problem, edged closer to him and nuzzled his hand. Kevin sank down and threw his arms around the dog's neck, clearly grateful for the offered comfort.

Dani knew she should be just as furious as the constantly outraged father they described. Her entire morning's work had been destroyed. Given what she herself had done to the bread, it was going to be a costly waste.

And yet as she had watched the sibling drama unfold and listened to the rush of excuses and teary-eyed plea for mercy, a huge empty space deep inside her filled with longing.

Forget who was to blame, forget the ruined pies, she couldn't bring herself to scold either one of them. This was exactly the sort of mischief she'd meant to be surrounded by by this time in her life. Her heart turned to mush just staring at those blueberry-covered faces and their protective, mixed-breed dog.

Not that immediate leniency would do, of course. A responsible adult would at least make them sweat a little longer before offering forgiveness. Besides, punishment was probably meted out on a regular basis by their father and it clearly hadn't had any effect whatsoever. Only now did it strike her that there had been no mention of a mother. For the first time it occurred to her just who these boys might be.

"Tell me your names," she said, fixing her gaze on the oldest boy first. "You are?"

"Timmy Watkins," he admitted readily enough.

"And I'm Kevin," his brother chimed in.

Watkins. The name instantly rang a bell. For the past few weeks she'd been hearing about two out-of-control newcomers to Riverton named Watkins. They were sons of a widower, who apparently didn't know the meaning of discipline, according to those who'd already had run-ins with them. They were a very poor reflection on their dear great-grandparents, claimed those who remembered Seth and Wilma with fondness.

She'd been told the boys were a pint-size demolition force. In fact, her neighbor swore she had seen the littlest one driving his father's pickup right before it smashed into the railing outside Stella's Diner, shattering the wood into splinters. Another friend, who lived on the opposite side of town, swore they were responsible for the destruction of her vegetable garden. If even half of what she'd heard was true, today's mischief appeared to be all in a typical day's work for the pair.

"Are you going to tell our dad?" Timmy asked.

Before Dani could reply, his expression turned stoic. "I guess you have to, huh? Grown-ups always stick together."

For once Dani decided not to fall into the trap of doing the expected. "What do you think I should do?" she asked. It was her experience that kids were often far tougher on themselves than any adult would ever be inclined to be. It would be fascinating to see how these two meted out justice.

Clearly intrigued by her willingness to take suggestions, Timmy said eagerly, "You could make a pact with us. We'd make you our blood brother.

Well, sister, I guess. That way it could be our secret forever.''

She gave the proposal some thought, then nodded. ''That is one possibility, I suppose. Any other ideas?''

''And we would promise never, never to do it again,'' Kevin offered.

''A promise would be good,'' Dani agreed.

''We'd write it all out and sign in blood,'' he added enthusiastically.

''And exactly what would you be promising not to do again?'' inquired a lazy, sexy male voice that could have melted an entire blizzard's worth of snow. Even the dog went crazy at the sound of it, running around the yard in excited circles again.

''Ohmigosh,'' Kevin muttered. ''We're dead.''

Based on their reactions, Dani gathered that that beguiling voice belonged to their father, a veritable ogre from their descriptions of his frequent wrath. He didn't sound like any ogre she'd ever imagined.

She glanced up from the two pint-size hellions who'd been terrorizing Riverton, Wyoming, for the past month and found herself face-to-face with the most incredibly gorgeous, thoroughly male human being she had ever set eyes on. All thoughts of pie and punishment fled.

Instead, she considered hurling herself straight into the muscular arms he had folded across his very broad chest. Blue eyes, a grown-up version of the boys', were the exact shade of a cloudless Wyoming sky. Blond hair, barely darker than his sons', and the same careless style should have made him look angelic. But, like Timmy and Kevin, this man appeared to know an awful lot about sin. Pure devilment glinted in those eyes. A woman would have had to be blind to miss it.

Of course, once he'd taken a thorough survey of the porch and added up two and two, he didn't seem to like the conclusion he reached. A little of that impudence faded. In fact, the weariness that settled onto his face said a lot about just how frequently he came upon situations exactly like this one. For whatever reason, he chose to deal with the barking dog first.

"Pirate, sit," he ordered, proving that someone with a sense of humor had named the dog based on the lopsided black patch surrounding one eye. Pirate obeyed at once, tongue lolling as he gazed adoringly at his master.

Mr. Watkins seemed grateful that at least someone in the family minded him. He patted the dog's head absentmindedly as he focused his attention on his sons.

"I assume you two are responsible for this," he said with an air of parental resignation.

"Yes, sir," Timmy said.

His father nodded at the expected admission, then turned his full attention on Dani.

"I'm Slade Watkins. As I suppose you've gathered, these are my sons," he said as if under the circumstances he very much regretted the fact.

At that precise moment Dani wouldn't have cared

if he'd admitted parenting Jack the Ripper. The effect of all that blatant masculinity directed her way was enough to make her knees go weak. Obviously it had been way too long since she'd met anyone with Slade Watkins's credentials in the masculinity department.

Now, for the very first time in her life, she understood what Sara and Ashley had been talking about when they'd described that pit-of-the-stomach excitement that they'd felt when they'd met their respective mates. It was a sensation she'd been virtually certain less than an hour ago that she would never experience.

She was so lost in thought, so caught up in the new sensations dazzling her that it took some time before she realized that Slade Watkins was talking to her.

"The boys will pay for the pies," he assured her, scowling at the two offenders.

His expression was daunting enough that any other child would have quivered with dread. Not these two, Dani noted with a measure of admiration.

Timmy straightened his shoulders with a touch of defiance. Despite his berry blue face and the accusations and counteraccusations being hurled only moments before, Kevin physically aligned himself with his brother. Side by side, they presented a united front.

"Why should we?" Timmy demanded, no longer nearly as accommodating as he'd been before his father's untimely arrival. "It's just some dumb old pies. They shouldn't have been out here on the porch in the first place. Whoever heard of putting pies outside or baking so many at once, anyway? She was practically begging somebody to take them.''

''You don't take what's not yours,'' Slade pointed out. ''I don't care where it is. Not only that, Ms. Wilde earns a living from baking these pies.''

Dani was startled by his awareness both of her identity and of the livelihood she made from selling baked goods, jams and canned fruits and vegetables through the nearby general store. Given the indecent prices tourists paid for these homemade, gourmet items, a few wasted pies were going to make very little difference in her overall income for the month. She was about to tell Slade Watkins exactly that when he caught her gaze. There was a grim, steely-eyed warning in his expression that kept her silent.

''What would each pie sell for?'' he asked.

''Ten dollars,'' she said in a rush. Okay, she was cheating a bit, but she couldn't charge these children what some tourist would have paid. Even at the cut rate, the two wide-eyed boys stared at her in dismay.

''Ten whole dollars?'' Timmy asked incredu-lously. ''For each one?''

''Actually, I think she's giving you the wholesale price,'' Slade Watkins told his son. ''The sticker in the store says fifteen.''

''But, Dad, that's our whole allowance for the next two years, probably,'' Kevin protested. ''Timmy's and mine. We won't even be able to play a video game or rent a movie or anything."

"You should have thought of that before you walked onto this porch."

"We just wanted to taste one," Kevin whispered. "We haven't had homemade pie since Mama—"

Slade Watkins cut him off as if the mention of their late mother was impossible to bear. "That is not the point. If you wanted pie, you should have told me."

"Like you can bake," Timmy muttered.

"I could have bought one of these," Slade pointed out. "That is, if you hadn't ruined them all." His gaze returned to Dani. "How many were there?"

That look on his face demanded the truth, not another of her fibs. "A dozen," she confessed.

"That's like a hundred dollars or something," Timmy said, clearly stunned.

"A hundred and twenty," his father corrected. "I'd say you're going to be very busy this summer earning extra money to pay off your debt."

Shock spread across Kevin's round face. "But, Dad, we're just little kids. You can't make us get jobs."

"No, but I can give you chores," he said sternly. "Lots and lots of chores. So many chores that you'll fall into bed exhausted every single night and won't have one minute left over for mischief."

Despite Slade's forbidding expression and his un- spoken warning not to interfere, Dani took pity on the boys. They hadn't meant any real harm. They couldn't have known these pies were her livelihood. They'd just missed their mother's baking. Her heart ached for them.

"Perhaps we could work out an arrangement," she said as two pairs of hopeful eyes instantly fixed on her. "You could do some chores for me to earn the money."

Their expressions brightened at once. Clearly they felt that she'd be a far less stern taskmaster than their father. They probably figured they could con her out of a share of baked goods, too.

"Like what?" Timmy asked.

Since she hadn't actually thought it through before making the impulsive offer, she improvised. "Well, I never seem to have enough time to do what needs doing around here. The porch needs sweeping again right this minute, for one thing. The windows probably should be washed. I never did get to my spring cleaning this year. And somebody has to clean up all these blueberries before they stain the wood."

They eyed the porch dubiously. There was no mistaking what a daunting task that would be.

"It might even need painting," Timmy suggested unhappily. "Dad doesn't let us paint."

"Not since you spray-painted the dog," he agreed. He gazed at Dani. "I appreciate what you're trying to do, but I really don't think this is such a good idea. You can't possibly know what you're—"

Dani cut him off before he could say another discouraging word. "Of course I do, and it's a wonderful idea," she said. "Extra pairs of hands are always welcome."

"I think these hands will be more of a hindrance than a help," he said.

"Let me worry about that," she insisted. "I think Timmy, Kevin and I understand each other. I'll enjoy having them here." She glanced at the dog. "Pirate, too, of course."

Slade Watkins actually gaped at that.

Dani returned his startled expression with an amused look of her own. She doubted anyone in Riverton had volunteered to spend so much as a second more than necessary with his boys. Left unspoken was the fact that she craved the noise and confusion these two imps would bring into her too-quiet house. How could she explain a thing like that to this man who seemed totally bemused by that very same mischief?

"Dad, would that be okay?" Timmy asked. "*Please.* We'd do whatever she says. You were going to have to find somebody to baby-sit us soon, anyway. You said so yourself. You said we couldn't be left to our own devices one more minute."

He was clearly echoing his father's precise words. Slade Watkins looked too chagrined not to have said exactly that, and quite recently.

"I'm sure you would be very helpful," Dani said, cheerfully agreeing with Timmy. "Really, Mr. Watkins, they'd be just fine with me."

"I'm less concerned with their welfare than yours," he said.

"No need to worry about that," she assured him. "I adore children."

"They're something of a handful," he added, as if she needed reminding of that.

Talk about an understatement! Yet he sounded so weary that Dani immediately wanted to throw her arms around him and tell him everything would be all right.

This was the role she'd been born to play—mother, wife, nurturer. Never before had she seen a man or children so in need of what she had to offer. Never had she felt this quickened pace of her pulse just gazing into a man's eyes or hearing his voice. She wasn't going to let the three of them disappear from her life so easily.

Even as the implication of those thoughts registered, an outrageous idea began to take shape. As bold as anything Sara or Ashley had ever considered, she was sure, the idea began to blossom.

Pure happenstance had caused their paths to cross, though in a town the size of Riverton that would have happened eventually, she supposed. But this particular set of circumstances, which suggested that these boys desperately needed more supervision than their widower father could give them, struck her as fortuitous.

She didn't have to be smacked over the head to recognize that perhaps Slade Watkins and his two boys were the opportunity she'd been waiting for practically forever, it seemed. Maybe everyone who had known her her whole life long had tucked her into a quiet, boring niche, but she hadn't spent all those years around sassy Sara and bold Ashley without learning a few things. Reaching out and grabbing on to a dream was at the top of the list.

Her dream—a little messy at the moment and a little intimidating from the looks of the three males before her—finally appeared to be within her grasp.

How, though, could she make that happen? How could she convince a virtual stranger that she was the answer to his prayers?

Well, she didn't have to do all of her convincing today, she concluded. She just had to get Slade Watkins to agree to this first step.

"You won't find anyone in town who'll take better care of the boys," she promised him.

He eyed her warily, clearly not convinced. "How did we go from them working off their debt to you taking care of them? You're volunteering to do what I would be paying an arm and a leg to someone else to do. As it is, I already owe you for all those pies."

She waved off the transition as if it were of no consequence, a mere matter of semantics. Stepping off the porch, she deliberately reached for two berry-stained hands. With Timmy on one side of her and Kevin on the other, they gazed into Slade Watkins's grim face.

"It will be just fine," she promised him one more time. "All the work Timmy and Kevin will do around here will more than make up for the pies."

Slade looked doubtful, but Timmy and Kevin nodded solemnly. Even Pirate seemed to approve of the plan. He nosed his way between Dani and Kevin for a united front. Slade wiped his hand across his eyes, then sighed heavily.

"If you're sure..."

"I am," she said staunchly.

Relief and worry warred in his expression, but relief won. He held out his hand.

"I appreciate your taking this so well," he said solemnly. "Some people, well, a lot of people wouldn't have been so understanding."

Dani couldn't think of anything to say at all. She was too busy wondering why she'd never known that a man's touch could set off fireworks more glorious than any the town had ever shot off on the Fourth of July.

"Will eight o'clock tomorrow morning be okay?" he asked.

She had to shake herself before she could imagine what on earth he was talking about.

"Oh, yes," she said, fighting the breathless sensation washing over her. In fact, she thought, eight o'clock couldn't possibly come soon enough.

Chapter Two

"I heard the terrors of Riverton struck," Sara said, settling down at Dani's kitchen table to watch as Dani started a fresh batch of pies later that afternoon. "How could any descendents of Seth and Wilma be such brats?"

"Don't call them that," Dani retorted sharply as she scooped blueberries into the crusts. "People live up—or down—to what's expected of them."

Sara's perceptive gaze narrowed. "You sound awfully defensive about two kids who destroyed an entire morning's work. What's that all about?"

Before Dani could respond, her sister's expression shifted from bemusement to sudden understanding. "Wait, wait, I get it. They're kids, right? Your huge, soft heart went pitter-pat just at the sight of them, even though they were covered from head to toe in your blueberries.''

Dani winced at the all-too-accurate assessment. "So, kill me. I'm a sucker for children. There are worse traits. How did you hear about this, anyway?''

"Myrtle Kellogg next door saw the whole thing. After that, she had lunch at Stella's.'' Sara shrugged. "It's only a short hop from there to the entire universe. I heard about it from Ashley, who had heard every detail by twelve-fifteen from Dillon, who'd stopped for coffee at Stella's. He couldn't wait to call home and fill in our baby sister.''

"The Riverton grapevine lives,'' Dani muttered, uncertain why she'd thought for a minute the incident would go unnoted. At least no one knew about the plan she intended to set into motion to make those darling boys—and their father—her own.

"So, what's he like?'' Sara asked.

Dani stared at her blankly. "Who?''

"Slade Watkins, of course. I barely remember him visiting. I heard he grew up to be a hunk, even if he does let his children run wild. According to our dear brother-in-law, poor old Myrtle could hardly catch her breath, she was so overcome by the sight of him.'' She regarded Dani speculatively. "What about you? Were you overcome, too?''

Denying that she'd noticed anything at all about Slade Watkins would be about as believable as saying she could hardly wait to go hunting for moose. "He is rather nice-looking,'' she admitted, praying that she'd struck just the right balance between truth and nonchalance.

"Nice-looking," Sara mimicked. "Gracious, Dani, if you can't tell the difference between gorgeous and nice-looking, maybe you ought to take that free eye examination the doc is offering."

Dani sighed. "Okay, he's gorgeous. Satisfied?"

Sara grinned. "Then you did notice. Good." She propped her elbows on the table and leaned forward intently. "Does he meet the Danielle Wilde daddy-factor test?"

The probing personal question was irksome, but unavoidable. Her sisters had been on the lookout for someone just like Slade Watkins for her for years. "Shouldn't you be home chasing cattle around the range or something?" Dani grumbled.

"Ah, an evasive answer. I love it!" Sara gloated. "Maybe Jake and I ought to be neighborly and invite Slade Watkins to a family dinner at the ranch so he can get reacquainted with Daddy and Ashley and Dillon."

The very thought made Dani shudder. She leaned down and peered directly into her sister's sneaky, laughing eyes. "You do and you're a dead woman."

Sara's expression turned innocent. "Of course, you could come, too, if you're interested."

"I'm warning you," Dani said. "No cozy little dinners. No getting-to-know-you chats. No one really remembers Slade anyway and you know it. Stay out of this."

"Out of what? I'm just trying to be friendly."

"Fiddle-faddle," Dani retorted succinctly. "You're meddling. You're turning out to be worse than Daddy. Ever since you and Jake got hitched, you've been blissfully determined to see the rest of us settled down, too. Be satisfied that Ashley and Dillon are married and let it go at that."

"Are you saying you're no longer interested in having a houseful of kids?"

"Of course not."

"Well, then, what's wrong with nudging that along a little? You have to admit Slade Watkins is the most likely candidate to stride into Riverton in years. He's a widower. He has two cute-as-the-dickens little boys who've obviously already stolen your good sense and your heart, despite their obvious character flaws. Marrying him would be a whole lot better than marrying one of the candidates Daddy's dreamed up for you."

"Maybe so, but I can handle my own love life, thank you very much."

Sara regarded her skeptically. "I haven't seen any evidence of that up until now. When was the last time you actually had a date? And don't count lunch with Horace to discuss how many pies to bake for his store."

For a fleeting instant Dani almost longed for her father's interference. At least she had learned to tell him to butt out. Sara was harder to dislodge than a burr. She sighed and tried to exhibit a little patience. The more she balked, the longer Sara was likely to stay.

"Like you just said, there haven't been any candidates around worth mentioning."

Sara's expression turned triumphant. "Then you do agree that Slade Watkins has potential?"

Unfortunately, persistence was a trait shared by all three of the Wilde sisters. "If I do, will you go home?" she pleaded.

"Naturally," Sara said. "I'll have what I came for—insider information."

Dani waved her spoon threateningly under her sister's nose. "And you know what happens to people who share insider information, don't you?"

"What?"

At first Dani couldn't think of anything quite dire enough to terrify her sister into silence. She eventually settled for telling her that she would happily put a bug in Trent Wilde's ear that Sara and Jake were about to make him a grandparent. Horror spread across her sister's face.

"You wouldn't dare," Sara said.

"Oh, but I would," Dani assured her. "Just imagine how Daddy will be plaguing you two for news about the impending big event. He'll probably take up a post outside your bedroom door to make sure you and Jake are working on the project. He won't let it rest until you've delivered the perfect grandbaby. You've already been married a year. He thinks it's way past time for you to produce an heir. He'll be so excited to know you're trying that he'll start passing out cigars in town. Everyone in Riverton will know the details of your sex life. Are you beginning to get the picture of the misery your life will become?''

"Yes, sister dearest, you've made your point."

Satisfied that Sara was suitably impressed with the consequences of blabbing a single word about Dani's interest in Slade Watkins, Dani grinned. "So, do I have your word that nothing leaves this room?"

Sara solemnly crossed her heart. "On my oath to Jake that we will wait at least another year before having a baby. Now, talk."

"Slade Watkins makes my knees go weak," Dani confessed.

Her sister bounced out of her seat and threw her arms around Dani. "Oh, sweetie, I'm so glad for you. It's about time."

"Way past time, if you ask me."

"Does he know how you feel?"

"Sara, I just met the man this morning. Other than talking about his sons, we barely said two words."

"When are you seeing him again?" Sara asked. When Dani didn't respond, she demanded, "You are seeing him again, aren't you? Tell me you didn't let this opportunity slip through your fingers."

"I certainly did not. I'm seeing him tomorrow," Dani finally admitted.

"Well, hallelujah!"

Lest her sister get too carried away, she added, "He's dropping the kids off at eight."

Sara looked thunderstruck. "You're baby-sitting those terrors?"

"Sara," Dani warned.

"Sorry, but I can't believe you've actually invited them back here without seeing to it that they've been put through some sort of military school regimen to break their wild little spirits."

"Their wild little spirits, as you put it, are what I love about them. Besides, they're working off the damage they did," Dani said defensively.

Sara's expression turned thoughtful. "And you'll be seeing a lot of their father. I take it back. That's ingenious. Subtle. You don't want to scare him off by appearing too eager. Dani, it's perfect."

"This isn't just some scheme to lure Slade Watkins back here. I like the boys," Dani argued. "They're sweet."

"If you say so."

"I want them here."

"Uh-huh."

"Go home, Sara."

Sara dutifully headed for the door.

"And keep your mouth shut."

"I promised, didn't I?"

"I know exactly how persuasive and sneaky Daddy can be when he wants information," Dani reminded her. "If you heard about this morning, he will have, too. He'll have questions. He'd better not get answers from you. One word crosses your lips and the talk at Sunday dinner will turn to babies. I guarantee it."

Sara looked suitably impressed with the repeated warning, but Dani knew her father as well as anyone on earth. If he couldn't wrangle anything out of Sara when she got home, he'd be on Dani's doorstep in the morning. Fortunately, years of ranching had made him an early riser. With any luck, he'd come and go before Slade Watkins showed up with the boys. It was certainly something worth praying for.

Naturally her prayers fell on deaf ears. Slade was in the process of admonishing the boys to be good—for the tenth time—when Trent Wilde pulled to a stop at the curb in front of Dani's house promptly at eight the next morning. His smirking expression as he exited his four-wheel-drive vehicle set her teeth on edge. Given the impeccable timing of his arrival, she vowed to throw Sara and Jake's time-table for baby-making to the wolves. In the mean-time, she had her father to deal with.

"Hello, Daddy," she said, kissing his cheek. Then she added pointedly, "I wasn't expecting you."

"Since when can't a father pay a surprise visit to his daughter?" he inquired distractedly, most of his attention already focused on her company. "You must be Slade Watkins. I knew your grandparents. I've been hearing a lot about you lately."

"I'm sure," Slade said dryly. "And I'd wager these two are the cause of most of it."

"Mr. Watkins, this is my father, Trent Wilde," Dani said. "He used to be a rancher. Now he spends his retirement meddling."

Slade grinned. It was the first time Dani had seen

anything resembling a smile on his face and it was enough to weaken not just her knees, but her spine. What it did to other parts of her anatomy made her breathless.

"That's what fathers do," he reminded her, then glanced at his sons. "Right, boys?"

"Yes, sir," Timmy said, though most of his attention was reserved for Dani's father, who was wearing his favorite handmade snakeskin boots, pressed jeans, a Western-cut shirt and his best Stetson in honor of this opportunity to meet Dani's potential beau.

Kevin was staring, as well. "Are you a real cowboy, sir?"

"Some would say so," Trent said, hunkering down in front of him. "You interested in being a cowboy?"

"Do you have to ride a horse?"

"Quite a lot," her father said.

Kevin's eyes widened. "Really? Wow, that's the best. I want to learn to ride."

"Sure you do, squirt," Timmy said with big-brotherly skepticism. "You're scared of horses."

"Am not."

"Are, too."

"You're the one who's chicken."

"Boys," Slade said softly. "Enough." He glanced worriedly at Dani for about the hundredth time since his arrival. "Are you sure...?"

"We'll be just fine," she promised. Pirate woofed

his agreement in that bizarre, husky tone he had, then settled down in a patch of sunlight nearby.

Slade handed her his business card. "You can reach me anytime. I can be here in ten minutes or less."

"That won't be necessary, I'm sure."

Her father's intent gaze was fixed on Slade. "You work close by?"

"Actually, I work at home. I'm a computer software designer."

"He's the best," Timmy said with unmistakable pride. "You should see some of the stuff he's created. It's awesome. I've only beat one of his games once. Kevin can't beat them at all. And everybody says we're computer whizzes."

"I just do those games for you guys," Slade reminded them. "I get paid for designing business and investment programs."

"Fancy that," Trent said.

He looked a little too fascinated for Dani's liking. She jumped in. "Well, I'm sure Mr. Watkins would like to get to work, Daddy. We should let him go."

Amusement lit her father's eyes. "Don't rush the man off, Dani. We were just getting acquainted." He turned back to Slade. "I can't say that I know too much about computers, but I'd be mighty interested in seeing what you do sometime."

Before Slade could reply, he added, "Maybe now, if it's not too much of an imposition."

The very thought of her father going off with

Slade Watkins made Dani's blood run cold. "You can't," she blurted at once.

Both men stared at her.

"Why the devil not?" her father demanded.

Heaven help her, Dani thought, as she said, "Because I need you here."

Her father seemed intrigued by that, especially since she'd been declaring her independence from him for the past decade. She hadn't accepted so much as advice on snow shoveling in all that time. Not that that had kept him from offering unsolicited advice on every subject imaginable.

"Really?" he said. "To do what?"

"You can supervise while the boys scrub the porch."

Her father's eyes sparkled with merriment. "That would be the porch stained with blueberries?"

"That's the one."

He turned back to Slade and shrugged. "I guess we'll have to do it another time."

Dani noticed that Slade appeared almost as relieved as she was. Apparently he'd detected all those fatherly undercurrents, too.

"You're welcome anytime," he assured her father politely before his gaze settled on Dani again. "Are you sure…?"

"If you ask me that one more time, I'm going to be insulted," Dani told him. "Go on to work and don't worry about a thing. Anything I can't handle, I'm sure Daddy can." She shot a pointed look at her father. "He's always wanted a houseful of little boys to mold in his own image."

"I'll be back by five," Slade promised. "Unless you need me before then."

"Five will be just fine," she said, wondering how she'd live through the hours until she caught the next glimpse of him. Lordy, but just the sight of the man was addictive. What would happen if they turned out to be compatible, too? Her body would probably go up in flames from internal combustion.

When Slade had finally departed with obvious reluctance, her father gazed at her. "Interesting man, wouldn't you say?"

"Yes," Dani said, then briskly turned her attention to the boys. "Let's get busy with the porch, shall we?" She beamed at her father. "Daddy, I was serious. You can supervise."

"I figured you made that up just to keep me from chasing after your young man."

Dani shot a worried look at the boys. Fortunately they weren't paying any attention. They were trying to coax Pirate into chasing a Frisbee.

"Slade is not my young man."

"Whatever," her father said. "At any rate, I thought I'd run on over to visit Ashley for a bit. See how things are coming with that fool business she's started up. Whoever heard of making money by teaching women how to fix their faces?"

If Dani had ever suffered from sibling rivalry or a desire for revenge, she would have let him go, but she figured her sister deserved a break just this once.

Besides, keeping him here might break the gossip chain, at least until suppertime when he went back to the ranch.

"I need you here," she insisted.

"In a pig's eye," he retorted. "But I'll stay." He grinned at the boys, who'd given up on getting Pirate's attention. "Can't have a woman getting herself all mussed up doing men's work, can we?"

Timmy and Kevin seemed intrigued by the notion that the scrubbing they were about to do qualified as "men's work." Dani left the three of them with buckets of sudsy water, stiff brushes and the hose. Pirate finally roused himself from his spot in the sun and began racing through the showers of water, barking his fool head off. The noise was deafening...and wonderful.

When Dani came back to check on them an hour later with milk and fresh-baked cinnamon rolls, she found all of them soaking wet from head to toe. Her father looked more bedraggled than she could ever recall seeing him. He usually prided himself on his dapper appearance. As for the porch, the supposed object of all their energy, it looked only marginally better.

"It's going to take some paint," Timmy told her excitedly. "Uncle Trent says we can pick any color we want."

"*Uncle Trent* said that, did he?" She regarded her father sweetly. "Did he stop to consider what kind of taste you two boys might have?"

Her father winced at that. "We won't do anything

too outlandish, will we, boys? Maybe a nice bright yellow.''

"Yeah," Kevin said. "Yellow's a really happy color.''

Her father squeezed Kevin's shoulder. "Then yellow it is." He beamed at Dani. "Haven't had this much fun in a long time. Come on, boys. Let's get on over to the hardware store.''

"Before we have cinnamon rolls?" Timmy asked plaintively, eyeing the tray that was still in Dani's hand.

"Well, of course not," her father told him. "I can't imagine what I was thinking of. Grab a few and we'll eat 'em as we walk over there. That'll keep our energy up for sure.''

Dani watched the three of them head off down the street. The six-foot-two rancher and his two pint-size companions made quite a picture. They hadn't gone far when Dani realized something about herself she'd never known before. She was capable of deep, gut-wrenching jealousy. She wanted those boys to be chattering excitedly to her, not her father.

She reminded herself sternly that it was just one day. And there was a good reason for putting them into her father's capable hands. It was to keep him, not the boys, out of mischief.

She stood back and stared at the porch and tried to envision it being bright yellow. It would be…colorful, she concluded.

And happy, just as Kevin said. She was smiling by the time she went back inside.

* * *

"It's awfully quiet in here," Slade observed suspiciously when he returned promptly at five that evening. He looked as if he'd expected to find the house burned down or, at the very least, in ruins. "Where are the boys? Did you tie them up and gag them?"

"They're taking a nap," Dani told him. "They were completely tuckered out from painting the porch. Or maybe it was from the fumes of all the turpentine it took to get the yellow paint off them afterward."

Slade's blue eyes widened. "You actually let them paint the porch?"

"Daddy supervised—in a manner of speaking, anyway. He has some surprisingly lax ideas about supervision. He sure wasn't that way when we were growing up. He told me he was encouraging their creativity."

"Oh, God," Slade moaned. "What did they paint?"

"Aside from the porch?"

"Exactly."

"I believe the petunias are now yellow. And you might want to check Pirate for any lingering traces of the flower they tried to paint on his back. I curbed their little imaginations before they could touch up my hubcaps."

"Dear heaven. No wonder you convinced them to take naps. I'm surprised you didn't knock them out."

"I didn't convince them, exactly," she admitted.

"They sat down to look at a video and the next thing I knew, they were out on the sofa. Should I wake them?"

"Heavens, no," Slade said.

He said it with such heartfelt fervor that Dani chuckled. "They don't give you much of a break, do they?"

"They're just young and energetic, I know," Slade said. "But sometimes I swear they were put on this earth just to exhaust me."

"Well, take a break now. I baked cookies earlier. Have some." She put the plate on the kitchen table. "Milk or iced tea?"

"Iced tea would be terrific."

She poured him a glass, then sat across from him. "I'm sure most worn-out parents feel that way about their kids at one time or another," Dani said.

"But every day?" Slade asked.

"Maybe you should explain the concept of quiet time," she suggested.

"I did. That's why I bought them each a computer. I thought they'd sit there quietly and play the games I created. I made them practically impossible to beat, so they would be totally absorbed."

"Did it work?"

"They yell at the computer," he said wearily. "Then they race back and forth between their rooms to see if the other one is winning."

"Sibling rivalry," Dani suggested. "It's natural. They're also very protective of each other. You saw how they united to stand up for each other yesterday. That kind of loyalty at their age is terrific.''

He gazed across the kitchen table at her. ''Is that the way it is for you and your sisters?''

''Most of the time,'' she admitted with a grin. ''You haven't met Sara or Ashley yet, have you?''

''No, but the tales are legendary. I'm sure I even heard a few when I visited here as a kid. A few people have gone so far as to suggest that the three of you were every bit as bad as my kids.''

''Ashley and Sara, maybe,'' Dani said with a grin. ''Not me. I was an angel.''

He surveyed her intently, then said softly, ''I can believe it.''

Dani shivered all the way to her toes. Swallowing hard, she asked, ''Do you have brothers or sisters?''

''No. Maybe that's why I'm constantly amazed by the mischief the boys get into. I was a quiet, only child.''

''A computer nerd,'' Dani said, regarding him with skepticism.

''Yep.''

''You don't look like any computer nerd I ever met,'' she said before she realized exactly what she was saying. Embarrassment flooded her cheeks with color.

Slade laughed. ''Have you known many?''

''Now that I think about it, you're actually the first I've seen. In person, anyway. Computers have been slow coming to Riverton. People around here believe in doing things the old-fashioned way.''

"Still adding and subtracting with an abacus?" he teased.

"Not exactly," she quipped right back. "We discovered the calculator recently. It's improved the quality of life quite a bit."

He winked at her. "Just wait until I teach you all the tricks a computer can do."

Dani seriously doubted that learning computer skills would be half as instructional as an hour or two in private with Slade Watkins. Her imagination went into overdrive considering what she could discover with his lips on hers and her hands exploring that fascinating expanse of chest. She flushed just thinking about it.

Unfortunately, her straying thoughts caused her to miss whatever it was Slade had said.

"Hmm?" she murmured.

"I asked if you'd like to have dinner with us tonight," he repeated. "I could give you a crash course."

"A crash course?" she repeated blankly.

"In computers. I suspect sooner or later the boys are going to want to drag their laptops over here. You'd better have some idea what they're up to."

"Oh." She tried to keep the disappointment out of her voice.

"Is Dani coming to dinner tonight?" Kevin inquired sleepily, coming over to stand beside his father.

"I've asked," Slade told him. "She hasn't answered."

"Please," Kevin said, regarding her hopefully.

With two pairs of blue eyes focused on her, Dani couldn't have refused if her life depended on it. Not that she wanted to in the first place.

"Well, of course I'll come for dinner," she said.

"Will you bring dessert?" Kevin pleaded. "Daddy can't cook worth a lick."

"You haven't starved yet," Slade retorted indignantly.

"Almost," Timmy said from the doorway. "If we're having Dani over, maybe we should order pizza."

Slade looked at Dani sheepishly. "Exactly what I had in mind. Is that okay?"

She laughed. "Given the reputation of your cooking, I'd say pizza would be perfect."

and widened until by the time she had been in the terrible accident that ultimately took her life, they were merely coexisting. The boys had been the glue that held them together. For their sakes, he and Amanda had kept up a sad front until her tragic death.

Oddly, now that she was gone, he missed her in unexpected ways. He realized that despite their differences, despite her wandering attention and frequent affairs, Amanda had provided something he needed and had no idea how to create for himself— a home.

He glanced around the old Victorian house he'd visited only a few times as a child and tried to put a finger on exactly where he'd fallen short. The rooms were bright and airy. The furniture was exactly the same as it had been in the Denver home he and Amanda had shared, albeit a little dustier. There were even a few remnants of his grandparents' belongings, genuine family heirlooms.

Goodness knew, the house looked lived in, he thought as he snatched up a handful of recently laundered underwear that had never made it past the sofa. And it was as charming as he'd remembered, a fact which had lured him back when Denver had begun to feel claustrophobic after Amanda's death.

Even with the evening sun splashed across the polished wood floors and a soft breeze filtering through the sheer curtains, it lacked something. Maybe Danielle Wilde, whose house practically radiated a friendly, inviting, homey atmosphere, could help him pin it down.

Despite that hopeful thought, he wished he hadn't impulsively uttered the invitation for tonight. Now he was stuck with it, an endless evening of trying to make conversation with a woman he barely knew.

His only consolation was that the boys were ecstatic. They had even eagerly agreed to help him straighten the place up before her arrival. Of course, their idea of tidying up consisted of tossing everything into the nearest closet, a habit they'd no doubt learned from him. Thank goodness it was summer and there would be no need to hang up their guest's coat and risk a tumbling of hidden clutter.

He took another quick survey of the downstairs and nodded. "I guess that does it." He called the boys, who came clattering down the stairs the very first time, for a change. "Did you both wash up and change your shirts?"

Even as he asked, he realized he should have been able to tell without asking, at least about the shirts. Unfortunately, Kevin and Timmy's taste ran to multiples of the exact same T-shirt. Each of them had at least a half dozen, all in red, except for those that had accidentally fallen into a load of laundry with bleach. Having declared them dorky, they refused to wear the resulting pink shirts anyway.

A close inspection indicated that the clothes they had on now were indeed freshly laundered. Their faces were scrubbed. Even their hair had been plastered down with enough gel to hold it in place through a hurricane. He found their desire to impress Dani Wilde touching. That she had endeared herself to them so quickly was a surprise. For all of their high-spirited mischief, his sons were innately shy, just as he had been at their age.

He thought back to his own childhood. He'd had exactly the wrong sort of personality for the son of a blustery Texas rancher. It had been a bone of contention between them for years, until his father had required a little computer help to organize his growing business interests. Since then a grudging sort of respect had sprung up between them. Even so, it was easier on both of them if they simply avoided each other. He hadn't been back to Texas in years now. He missed his mother, but not much else.

He grinned at Timmy and Kevin. "You look very handsome," he assured them.

Relief spread across their faces. "You're sure?" Timmy asked.

"Very sure."

"She's coming," Kevin announced, racing toward the front door and slamming it open. Pirate dashed out, barking and leaping into the air, convincing Slade that he'd been a circus dog in some previous life or perhaps even before they'd picked him up from an animal shelter.

"Right here, Dani," Kevin shouted as if she weren't already parked in their driveway and being besieged by their dog.

Slade watched as both of his boys practically tumbled down the front steps as they ran to greet her.

Before he could wonder how she had conquered their hearts so easily, he saw her hunker down to their level and admire their slicked-back hair, their red shirts and their brand-new sneakers. She did it so naturally, so sincerely it made Slade's heart ache. That was it, of course. The boys craved a woman's praise, a woman's warmth and tenderness. They would have gravitated to any woman who offered it so freely.

He sighed as he watched the three of them. That was the one thing he could never give them, no matter how hard he tried. After he had failed so miserably to make Amanda happy, he had vowed never again to move into a relationship in which he would be so completely out of his depth. He understood the complexities of computers far more readily than he did those of women. There would never be another marriage. Never.

Perhaps, though, the boys would be content enough with a woman like Danielle Wilde in their lives, a surrogate mother who would generously give them all the things he couldn't. Of course, he was jumping to the conclusion that she would be willing to accept such a role in their lives.

He reassured himself that the conclusion was based on sound evidence. After all, she had welcomed them into her home without a qualm, even after that abysmal introduction and the destruction of all those pies. In fact, she had seemed so eager to have them around that Slade had almost felt as if he were doing her a favor, instead of the other way around.

He thought about that off and on all during dinner, as he silently sat back and watched her interaction with Timmy and Kevin. Why did a woman who so obviously adored children have none of her own? How had the men of Riverton missed noticing the way she lit up a room with her smile? Or the way light caught the sparks of red in her brown hair, giving it a rich, burnished sheen?

Slade shook off the unexpected and very male sensations stirring inside him. Surely this wasn't the reason he'd issued that impulsive invitation a few hours earlier. Surely he'd done it for his sons, not himself. Danielle Wilde was the last woman a man should consider having a fling with. As briefly as he'd known her, he recognized that she was all about permanence, all about settling down and forever.

No, she was definitely not the woman for him.

And yet, he couldn't deny that there was more laughter that night than he'd heard since they had moved into this beautiful old house. That, he finally realized with a sense of amazement, was what had been missing—the laughter.

He was stunned when he glanced at his watch and realized it was already after ten, well past the boys' bedtime and too late for the computer lesson that had been the ostensible reason for the invitation.

"Okay, you two, bedtime," he announced amid the expected groans and protests.

"It's summer," Timmy said. "There's no school tomorrow."

"But you do have a job now," Slade reminded them. "Ms. Wilde will expect you to be alert first thing in the morning." He glanced over to find her trying to hold back a don't-blame-this-on-me look.

"I guess we forgot," Kevin said. "Don't worry, Dani. We'll get all our chores done."

"I'm sure you will," she said complacently.

"Then will you let us play computer games?" Timmy asked. "We could teach one to you."

She looked properly aghast at the suggestion. "Play indoors on a lovely summer day? I don't think so. I was thinking it might be more fun if I invited some of the children down the street over for a picnic," she said casually, drawing wary looks from both boys.

"We don't know them," Kevin said, sounding hesitant.

Slade winced. He'd been so sure that waiting to move until the school year ended was the sensible thing to do. He hadn't stopped to think that school was where most children met their friends.

Not that either Timmy or Kevin were social creatures. They were too much like him, content to spend hours engrossed with their computers. Clearly, Dani had guessed that and was intent on changing it. He knew instinctively that she was right, that the boys needed to be encouraged to make new friends.

"A picnic sounds like a terrific idea to me," he

chimed in. "I envy you guys. I'll be shut away in here, while you're outside enjoying the sunshine."

"You could join us," Dani said at once, surprising him by seizing on his support. "I know you have to work and all, but my house is close by. It doesn't take more than a few minutes to get there. You could run over, eat and be back here almost as quickly as you could fix something for yourself."

Slade practically never ate lunch. He was usually too caught up in his work to even notice when noon came and went. But suddenly the rigidity of that single-minded focus grated. He pushed aside all thoughts of the impending deadline he faced.

"Are you sure you wouldn't mind my eating and running?"

"Absolutely not," she assured him with a smile.

"You'll really come, Dad?" Timmy said, looking awed.

"Absolutely. Now run along to bed. I'll be up to tuck you in in a half hour. Lights had better be out by then."

With obvious reluctance they took off, but only after hugging Dani. Kevin had whispered something in her ear that had made her smile.

After they were gone, Slade said, "You have yourself a couple of huge fans."

"They're wonderful boys."

"Even after what they did to you yesterday and to your petunias today, you can still say that? You're amazingly generous."

"Oh, for goodness' sakes, it was a few pies," she

said dismissively, "and a few flowers. It's not like they burned the house down."

"Give them time," Slade countered.

She chuckled at that.

"Hey, I'm serious. Don't let them out of your sight for a minute."

"I'm not worried," she said, though her expression contradicted it. "There is one thing I was wondering about, though."

"What's that?"

"They seemed to be nervous about meeting the other children in my neighborhood. Shouldn't I have suggested that?"

"Of course you should. They need to develop friendships. They used to have kids over all the time when they were younger." He thought back to when that had changed. He'd been blaming it on his own pattern of social ineptness, but he recognized suddenly that that was only a part of the problem.

"What is it?" Dani asked.

"I just realized that all that stopped after my wife's accident. They started sticking closer to home. Because she was in so much pain, we discouraged the boys from having their friends come by. Amanda was at home for nearly two months before she died." He rubbed his suddenly stinging eyes. "God, how could we have done that to them?"

The touch of Dani's hand on his shoulder was so gentle, so comforting that it stunned him to realize that it was also stirring a kind of wild anticipation that he had never expected to find again.

"You can't blame yourself," she said. "You had to do what was best for your wife. It must have been terrible for all of you. Believe me, I'm sure the boys will make friends quickly enough here, especially with their reputations for mischief. Kids their age are always eager for new ways to get into trouble."

Slade stared at her. "Is that supposed to reassure me?"

"Absolutely. The time to start worrying is when they're too quiet."

Her calm in the face of juvenile chaos awed him. Even women with children of their own had been daunted by his sons' wild behavior. "How did you get to be so smart about kids?" he asked.

"I surround myself with them as often as I can," she said with an oddly wistful note in her voice. "I borrow them from any parent who'll let me."

"I'm sure some, like me, are only too eager to turn over their little hellions."

"Not nearly as often as I'd like," she said with candor. "I always wanted a houseful of noise and chaos and laughter."

"I'm surprised you don't have it, then," he said. "Your family has a reputation for going after what it wants."

An odd expression crossed her face at that. Color bloomed in her cheeks, making her look more vulnerable and more desirable than ever. Slade realized then that he was going to be put to the test resisting her.

"Don't confuse me with Ashley and Sara," she reminded him. "I have my own ways of doing things."

"Which are just as effective, I'm sure," he said.

That odd look returned to her eyes briefly. Then she smiled as if she knew a grand and probably dangerous secret. "I certainly hope so."

Something told Slade he was better off not knowing exactly what she meant by that.

Dani had lured half a dozen boys over to the house to meet Timmy and Kevin. At the moment they were making a deafening racket in the backyard. She was loving every minute of it, though Myrtle Kellogg next door was hardly thrilled. She'd already called twice to complain. Dani had assured her the boys would settle down long before it was time for Myrtle to watch her soaps on TV.

"Your favorite's on at two o'clock, right?" She knew perfectly well it was, because the volume control on Myrtle's television rarely slipped below air-raid-warning decibels. Dani could practically hum the show's theme song in her sleep, she'd heard it so many times.

"I wouldn't like to do it, but I will call the sheriff, if I have to," Myrtle grumbled.

Dani thought her neighbor would probably like nothing better than doing exactly that, so she vowed to get the boys inside and silent by two.

Either that or she'd take them all to the park for an exuberant game of touch football. Maybe Slade would be willing to stick around and captain one team, while she led the other.

The thought of Slade's touch, even under such impersonal circumstances, was beginning to pop up so often that Dani wondered whether she'd be able to keep her own hands to herself much longer. She was almost certain that when she'd laid a comforting hand on his shoulder the night before, she'd felt a shuddering response wash through him. That had awakened all sorts of feelings of feminine power she hadn't experienced before. She was pretty sure that sort of adrenaline rush could become addictive, though.

"Okay, you guys," she called from the back door. "Time to help carry the food outside."

The immediate response was gratifying. She deposited bowls of potato salad and slaw into eager hands, along with plates of hamburgers ready for the grill, buns, slices of watermelon and a chocolate cake with fudge icing. Kevin carried the last with absolute reverence. She'd never seen him move so slowly or cautiously. He practically held his breath until he set it down on the picnic table in the yard. When Pirate came nosing around to check it out, Kevin pushed him back to a respectful distance and added a warning.

"You touch it and you're dead meat," he told the dog, who was practically quivering with excitement over all that chocolate.

Slade walked around the side of the house just as Dani placed the hamburgers on the grill. Her heart leapt into her throat at the sight of him. Was there any man on earth who could do for a pair of jeans what he did? It was downright sinful, and all the more fascinating because he seemed totally unaware of the effect.

"Nice timing," she said. "There's not even so much as a napkin left inside for you to carry."

He nudged her away from the grill with a bump of his hip. "Then let me take over here. Grilling is just about the only cooking I do with any evidence of talent."

"Yeah, if you like your burgers charcoal on the outside and raw meat inside," Timmy taunted.

Slade scowled at him. "Traitor."

"Dad, you taught us always to be honest," his older son said piously.

"Did you have to pick this precise moment to learn that lesson?" Slade grumbled.

Amused by the apparently familiar father-son bickering, Dani retrieved the spatula from his hand. "Maybe I'd better take over here. There are soft drinks in the cooler and iced tea in the pitcher on the table. If you'd rather have a beer, there's some in the refrigerator."

"Iced tea is fine. Beer would probably put me to sleep in front of the computer this afternoon."

Dani waited until he'd returned with his tea before she tossed out the idea she'd had just before his arrival. "Actually, I was wondering exactly how rigid your work schedule is. You are your own boss, right?''

Something flickered in his eyes, perhaps a reaction to her choice of words, she decided. Rigid. She'd chosen the word deliberately. Few people she knew liked to think of themselves as being inflexible, as being caught in a rut. Reminding him that he was supposed to be in charge of his own life was a nice touch, she thought.

''Why?'' he inquired a little testily, more or less confirming her guess.

''I was thinking maybe we ought to take the boys to the park after lunch for a touch football game. It would use up a little of that energy.'' Then she added the coup de grace. ''They might even take naps again this afternoon.''

She chuckled at his reaction. She doubted he would have looked any more shocked if she'd suggested a rendezvous in a cheap motel.

''You're kidding, right?''

''Absolutely not.''

Shock shifted to apparent fascination. ''And you're going to play?''

''Of course. I'll have you know I'm a very good receiver.''

His gaze promptly fell on her hands. Dani was very glad she'd thought to polish her neatly clipped nails the night before. Usually she spent so much of her time up to her elbows in flour that she didn't bother. Besides, what was the point of polishing nails that were trimmed nearly down to the quick for practical reasons? That dash of bright pink, however, did add a sexy touch to her workmanlike hands.

She waited until Slade's eyes met hers again before adding, "I have very strong hands."

His throat worked at that. "Oh, really?"

Obviously she'd sent his imagination soaring. It was a very gratifying reaction.

"It's all that kneading," she told him, adding to the color climbing up the back of his neck.

He shook his head as if to rid himself of the image, but his voice was still a little breathless when he asked, "I wonder if the coaches in the NFL ever thought to suggest their receivers ought to practice by making bread?"

"I doubt it, or some of them would be better than they are."

His growing curiosity was unmistakable. "Do you watch a lot of football?"

"In Trent Wilde's household, there wasn't a sport we didn't follow," she informed him. "My father's only regret was that he couldn't get any of us to turn pro. If he'd thought we were interested, he probably would have challenged the league rules on our behalf. Daddy really, really wanted—and expected—sons. He didn't cut us much slack for disappointing him by being girls."

Slade gestured toward the table and its burden of food. "Is that how you rebelled, by turning into a fabulous cook just to prove how feminine you are?"

She stared at Slade, surprised by his insight.

"Now that you mention it, I suppose it was. I never thought of it that way before." She grinned. "It does drive him crazy to find me with flour on my nose, instead of camouflage paint or something equally disgusting."

"Your father strikes me as a powerful man."

"In this state, he is."

"I didn't mean that. I was thinking of the force of his personality."

"That, too," she agreed. "And we all got our share of it. No one messes with a Wilde."

He grinned. "I'll remember that." He gestured toward the grill. "Now, are you ready for the hamburger buns, or don't you trust me with those, either?"

Dani did a slow and deliberate survey of him from head to toe, then nodded in satisfaction. "You look reasonably coordinated to me. You should be able to get them from there to here without any major catastrophes. When you get back, you can give me your answer about that touch football game."

A spark of pure mischief that equaled anything she'd seen in Timmy's or Kevin's eyes lit their father's.

"That's a foregone conclusion," he told her, his male pride clearly on the line. "It's the Watkins men against you and that ragged pickup squad of yours."

When Timmy and Kevin heard about the plans for after lunch, they gaped at their father.

"You're not going to work this afternoon?" Timmy asked.

"Nope," Slade said. "I never could resist a challenge, and Ms. Wilde has made certain that I couldn't turn her down. She actually thinks she and those other boys can beat the three of us."

Kevin stared at Dani, disbelief written all over his face. "You're going to play football, too?"

"Of course."

Both boys looked impressed. "I didn't know girls played football," Kevin said.

"Well, this one does," Dani assured him. "Any objections?"

"Heck, no," Timmy said. Suddenly he looked worried. "We don't have to tackle you, do we?"

Dani grinned. "I certainly hope you won't."

Slade groaned. "There goes the game."

She reached over and patted his cheek consolingly. "The outcome was always a foregone conclusion, anyway."

Apparently she'd gone a little too far with that taunt. Slade threw himself into the game with such enthusiasm that all of them were exhausted and filthy by the end of the afternoon.

Judging from the stunned and self-satisfied expression on his face, she gathered that despite all those taunts, he hadn't actually expected to win. She would never, not in a million years, tell him that she had deliberately dropped the pass that would have tied the score. He was savoring his victory too much.

"Are you going to gloat?" she inquired when

they were on the back porch with fresh glasses of iced tea, while the worn-out boys all lay collapsed on the grass. She hadn't felt so thoroughly content in a very long time. She could handle a little gloating.

"It wouldn't be polite," he told her.

She grinned. "No, but you really want to, don't you?"

He chuckled. "Yes, I do. I feel guilty as hell about it, but I do."

She sat up a little straighter, her expression deliberately stoic. "Go ahead. I can take it."

Before she realized that gloating was suddenly the last thing on his mind, he'd moved. His lips were on hers and, in deference to their audience, gone again. That quick brush with temptation was so startling, so thoroughly unexpected and intriguing that Dani's head reeled.

Eyes wide, she stared at him. If anything, his expression was more smug than it had been in victory.

"You're just full of surprises, aren't you, Slade Watkins?" she murmured.

He shrugged. "I'm beginning to think I just may be."

Judging from his tone, Dani wasn't certain which of them was more surprised by the discovery.

Chapter Four

Slade's eyes were blurring. He'd been staring at his computer screen ever since he'd dropped the boys off at Dani's, but for the first time in memory he couldn't seem to concentrate. He kept seeing images of Dani, her T-shirt damp and stretched taut over her breasts, her cheeks flushed with color, her hair tangled, her eyes sparkling with laughter as she leapt into the air to catch a poorly thrown pass. It had been over a week now and the fact that he couldn't shake that image terrified him.

He had never known a woman with so much exuberance or so little self-consciousness about what was proper. Even before her accident, Amanda would never have joined in an impromptu game of football with a bunch of rambunctious kids, much less instigated it. When she'd been home at all, she'd been more inclined to suggest a family evening in front of the TV with an old movie and a bowl of popcorn. It had allowed her to avoid any direct interaction with the husband she no longer loved.

Feeling an odd sort of loyalty to the woman who'd betrayed him, Slade warned himself to stop making comparisons. Amanda and Dani were two very different women and that was that. It didn't mean that Dani's way was right and Amanda's wrong.

It did seem to him, though, that he'd never felt more alive or more exhilarated than he had the previous afternoon when he'd tossed practical matters aside and done something totally impulsive. Seeing how thoroughly happy the boys were to have him there had reminded him that he'd left them to their own devices far too often for their good or his.

Not that he could quit working and play all the time, the way he felt like doing at the moment, he reminded himself. He tried to force his attention back to that blank computer screen. Nothing. Absolutely nothing came to him. The whole world of investments, which he normally found fascinating, today seemed totally uninspiring.

Fortunately, the chiming of his doorbell provided a welcome distraction. More often than not in the past, he would have ignored it, but today any interruption, even from a salesman, would be welcome.

Instead, though, he found Trent Wilde on his

doorstep. He had a sneaking suspicion this wasn't some sort of Riverton welcome call.

"Good morning," Dani's father said heartily. "Hope I'm not interrupting anything critical."

Despite his instinctive wariness at finding Dani's protective father on his doorstep, Slade was still glad of any interruption. "Hardly," he said. "I seem to be having trouble getting started today. Come on in. What can I do for you?"

"I thought maybe you could show me one of those fancy investing programs you made," Trent claimed. "Now that I've got all this time on my hands, I thought maybe I'd start managing my own portfolio."

He sounded sincere enough, but Slade's suspicions mounted. He couldn't imagine the rancher suddenly changing the way he'd handled investments all these years. More than likely, the powerful rancher was snooping for information about the new stranger in town, the stranger he'd discovered at his daughter's house a few days earlier. Being Seth and Wilma's grandson hadn't lifted him above suspicion there. He was going to have to earn the town's respect on his own.

Slade supposed he couldn't blame Trent for being a bit protective of a woman like Dani. Men were probably constantly trying to take advantage of her good nature and her family ties to a man who dominated so much of Wyoming's power broking.

"I'd be happy to show it to you," Slade told him, then gave him a general summary of the same reminder that appeared on the program's box. "But let me warn you, it's risky to take things out of the hands of a professional unless you have real experience with the stock market."

"A man's never too old to learn something new," Trent retorted. "Besides, it's my money to throw away, if I'm of a mind to."

Slade doubted the man before him had amassed so much land and wealth in Wyoming by throwing his money away, but he kept his impression to himself and led the way into his office. Trent's eyes widened at the state-of-the-art computer setup.

"This thing makes my little doodad look like a toy," he observed, running his hand over the mini-tower. He absentmindedly tossed his Stetson in the general direction of the sofa, then eagerly took Slade's seat in front of the screen.

"What's that for?" he asked, pointing to one slot in the front of the tower.

"A CD-ROM."

"You mean to play music?"

"It'll do that. Or you can get a whole interactive encyclopedia on CD-ROM, slide it in and look up whatever you want."

"Show me," Trent said, turning to face the screen.

Amused by his obvious fascination, Slade put the computer through its fancier paces. He rarely got to show off anymore, unless it was to the company that produced his programs, and they weren't nearly as awed by his skills as Trent Wilde obviously was.

"Well, I'll be. This thing's downright remarkable."

Delighted to have an enthusiastic audience, Slade broadened the demonstration to include some of his own latest programs. Trent's fascination never wavered. Slade's guard eventually dropped. That was why it was such a surprise when Trent glanced over at him and asked out of the blue, "You shown this to Dani yet?"

Warning bells sounded an alarm. "No, why?" he asked cautiously, wondering if he knew about Dani's visit for dinner a couple of nights earlier.

"It always seemed to me she ought to take up something practical as a career. She could learn a lot about computers from you—that is, if you wouldn't mind teaching her," he said with a sly look.

Slade recognized a master manipulator when he saw one. "I've already offered," he admitted, then added pointedly, "Of course, your daughter seems to have a mind of her own. She strikes me as a woman who's pretty content with her life just the way it is now."

"Baking bread and pies and canning summer vegetables is a crazy kind of a career, if you ask me," Trent scoffed. "She ought to be doing that for some man. If she wants a job, she ought to choose something substantial, something with a real future, like this. Computer skills would be a big help to her sister and Jake out at the ranch. I imagine Ashley would be able to use a little help in that area as soon as she has that new business of hers up and running. She tells me the reservations for her seminars are pouring in.''

Slade got the distinct impression it was an old argument between Trent Wilde and Dani over the direction of her life. He could just imagine the fireworks when the two strong-willed people locked horns. He wasn't about to get caught in the crossfire. Dani Wilde's decisions were none of his concern.

''Like I said, I offered to teach her the basics so she could play computer games with the boys, but beyond that it's not up to me to press her,'' he told her father.

Trent seemed ready to argue, but then his expression turned resigned. He sighed heavily at having his latest strategy thwarted. His disappointment was so obvious, Slade had to hide a smile.

''Now, if you wanted to learn a little more, I could try to find some time for a few lessons for you,'' he offered.

It was clear, though, that Trent had already covered the real purpose of his visit. He stood up. ''I'll let you know,'' he said as he grabbed his hat and strode from the room. At the front door he pinned Slade with a direct look. ''A man can get lonely in a small town like this.''

''I haven't so far,'' Slade responded.

''Well, if you do, be careful where you go looking for a distraction, if you catch my drift.''

If Slade hadn't already made the very same observation to himself about Dani, he might have resented her father's suggestion. He doubted, though, that Dani would have reacted as charitably to the blatant interference. For her sake, he forced a scowl.

"Your daughter is a grown woman. Don't you think she's capable of deciding what she does with her time or who she spends it with?" he asked bluntly.

Trent had the good grace to flush at the direct hit. That didn't stop him from adding, "None of my girls will ever get too old for me to stop looking out for their best interests." His stiff demeanor gave way to a rueful grin. "Not that they appreciate that much."

"I can imagine," Slade said.

"At least you and I understand each other, don't we?"

"We do, indeed."

Evidently satisfied that he had made his point, Trent strolled on out to his four-wheel-drive vehicle and climbed in. He drove off with a wave of his Stetson—and promptly turned not toward home but straight in the direction of his daughter's. Slade watched him go and tried to imagine how that confrontation was likely to go. He'd put his money on Dani any day.

Thoroughly frazzled and furious with her father, Dani was at her wit's end by the time Slade walked through the door that evening to pick up the boys. She hadn't even had time to run a comb through her hair—not that it would have made much difference given the way the humidity had put an extra bit of flyaway curl into it.

"Rough day?" Slade inquired, settling into what was becoming his usual place at the kitchen table. He looked as comfortable and at home as if he'd been dropping by for years, rather than just over a week.

"You can't imagine the half of it," she said with feeling.

"Oh? Did the boys do something more outrageous than usual?"

The question might have been perfectly innocent, but she doubted it. The glint in his eyes suggested he knew more than he was letting on, but she couldn't for the life of her imagine how. She was not about to fill him in on her father's annoying visit. It was just the latest in a long string of exasperating encounters, anyway. She ought to be used to his suggestions about her love life by now.

She forced herself to return Slade's curious look. "No," she reassured him. "Your sons were little angels, actually. They cleaned out the garage for me, top to bottom. I told them they could have a yard sale on Saturday and keep a percentage of whatever they made."

Slade grinned. "Ah, yes, the profit motive. They're starting early. Most kids begin with lemonade stands, though."

"The Bleecker boys will be selling lemonade," Dani told him. "And the Hinson twins are selling cupcakes."

"Sounds like quite an event. Who's making the lemonade and baking the cupcakes?"

"They are," she assured him. At his skeptical look, she admitted, "Okay, we're working on it tomorrow."

"Need any help? I'm not so hot with cupcakes, but I can probably manage to squeeze a few lemons."

Dani stared at him in surprise. "You'll help?"

"Why not? It sounds like fun."

He almost sounded as if he meant it, but the grimace on his face gave him away. She got the feeling he'd prefer sucking on a lemon to squeezing dozens of them.

"Never mind," she told him. "I can handle it. It'll be a picnic compared to some other things I can think of."

"Such as a visit from your father?" he asked, that glint of amusement back in his eyes.

Just as she'd thought, he did know. Her gaze narrowed. "How did you know about that?"

"You were his second destination this morning."

She groaned. "Don't tell me."

"I can see I don't need to. As you've already gathered, he dropped by my place first thing this morning, ostensibly to get a few computer tips. I got the distinct impression he was headed over here next. About eleven-fifteen, I'd say."

"Exactly."

"Was he pumping you for information or did he come bearing advice?"

She shrugged. "He usually does both."

"I don't suppose he mentioned anything about you learning computers so you could change careers."

Since Slade obviously already knew the gist of at least one aspect of her latest battle with her father, she sighed and sank into the chair opposite him. "Why can't he see that I am doing exactly what I want to be doing?"

"Because in his mind, real jobs are serious business. You strike him as having too much fun at yours."

"Do you suppose that's it? I hope so." Unfortunately that had been only a small part of her father's real mission. She regarded Slade worriedly. "He didn't get into anything else with you, did he?"

"Such as?"

The devilish gleam in his eyes was answer enough. She groaned. "He did, didn't he? He warned you to steer clear of me. Did he say anything about the two of us making a spectacle of ourselves in the park yesterday?"

Slade's outraged expression was answer enough, but he said, "We were playing touch football, for heaven's sakes."

"I know. The way he talked about it, you'd have thought we were mud-wrestling."

"Naked?" Slade inquired dryly.

"Exactly," she said. "What's wrong with him?"

"My hunch is he was indulging in a little reverse

psychology, hoping to throw us straight into each other's arms.''

"Oh, God," she whispered with a moan. She might be scheming the very same thing herself, but having her father in on the act was humiliating. He didn't know the meaning of subtlety.

"I thought it was kind of sweet," Slade offered by way of consolation.

She frowned at him. "Sweet, my hind end. He was meddling. It's his favorite pastime, now that he's retired. I told you that. I had hoped this little romance he's been carrying on lately with Matilda Fawcett would distract him."

"Who's Matilda Fawcett?"

Delighted to focus on somebody else's love life, Dani elaborated on her father's current flirtation. "Matilda Fawcett is the retired algebra teacher from Riverton High. Much to our amazement, my sisters and I have recently discovered that she and Daddy very nearly had a fling thirty-some years ago, even though she was his teacher at the time. All indications are that they are about to take up where they left off."

She sighed heavily. "I was so hoping he would. Or if not Matilda Fawcett, then maybe Annie, our housekeeper. Not that she'd have him. She knows him too well."

"In other words, you were hoping he'd be so busy he'd back off and leave you alone?"

"Precisely. You have no idea what it's like to have a father who's a control freak."

Slade's expression darkened. "I think I do," he said.

Something in his voice and the suddenly harsh lines of his face suggested that Dani had inadvertently wandered onto dangerous turf. "You, too?" she asked cautiously.

"Let's just say my father makes yours seem like a disinterested third party."

Dani's eyes widened. "Oh, my. I didn't know it was possible to be any worse than Daddy."

"That's because you haven't met Duke Watkins."

Still treading carefully because the subject obviously made him uncomfortable, she said, "You two don't get along?"

"Like oil and water." He shrugged. "Actually, it's not so bad anymore."

"Maturity set in?"

"No. I just haven't been anywhere near Texas for the past fifteen years."

Dani couldn't hide her shock. As aggravating as her father could be, she couldn't imagine him not being smack in the middle of her life. When he'd run off to Arizona a year or so before to kick up his heels, as he put it, she'd missed his drop-in visits and even his meddling more than she could say. One of the things she loved most about Riverton was that her family was all practically within shouting distance. Maybe they did make nuisances of themselves from time to time. It was a small price to pay for that sense of connection.

"You haven't seen your family in all that time?" she asked, thoroughly dismayed by the idea, even though Slade was clearly content with the arrangement.

"My mother came to visit once when Timmy was born, but after that she concluded the visits weren't worth the grief she took from my father."

Slade apparently caught her distraught expression, because he forced a smile. "Hey, don't look so sad. It's for the best. There's no point in spending time with folks if all you're going to do is butt heads and shout."

"But the boys don't even know their grandparents," she said impulsively. "That's the kind of relationship that gives kids a sense of continuity, of their place in the universe."

"I can't argue with that," Slade agreed. "But the situation my kids face is more the norm than not these days, what with the way people move around and divorce."

"I still think it's a shame, especially when it could so easily be changed," she said.

Before she could say more, Slade regarded her wryly and asked, "Now who's meddling?"

Dani was about to protest when she realized he was exactly right. She was meddling in something that was none of her business. It was just that she was already coming to think of Timmy and Kevin as an important part of her life. She had their best interests at heart. How awful that they had grandparents they'd never even met and undoubtedly knew very little about, judging from Slade's reticence on the subject.

It was awful for Slade, as well. Cutting ties with his family had to hurt more than he cared to admit. She resolved to see what she could do about getting him to mend fences. But not today. His forbidding expression warned her she would get nowhere.

She held up her hands. "I surrender."

An odd light flared in his eyes at her choice of words, then faded so quickly she was certain she must have imagined it. He looked as if he were preparing to bolt, so she quickly improvised an invitation that would assure them of spending some time together soon.

"I was thinking of taking the boys out to the ranch day after tomorrow, if that's okay with you."

"I suppose," he said after a very long hesitation.

Puzzled by his reaction, she asked, "Would you like to come along?"

"No," he said so sharply that Dani simply stared.

"Slade?" she said quizzically.

He stood up. "I'm sorry. It's time I got the boys home, or we'll never get dinner on the table."

Dani resisted the desire to suggest they stay and eat with her. She might want Slade Watkins and his boys to become her family, but it was far too soon for Slade himself to become aware of that. It would probably scare him to death or worse, cause him to view her as desperate and pitiful. No, now was not the time to press the issue.

"I baked an extra apple pie today. Would you like to take it home for dessert?"

At last his expression softened. "Now, you know perfectly well I can't say no to that. The boys would never forgive me. It'll probably be the only edible thing on the table."

She hesitated to bring it up again, since the last mention had nearly brought about an explosion of temper, but she wanted to be absolutely clear about what Slade's terse reply had meant.

"Are you sure you don't mind if the boys go to the ranch without you? I think they'll really enjoy it. They can learn to ride. Jake and Sara will both be around. So will Daddy, no doubt. They won't get hurt."

He looked torn, but he finally relented. "If they want to go, it's fine with me. Just don't expect me to come along."

Dani knew there was a story behind that, but she wisely refrained from pressing the issue. For the moment she had his commitment to let the boys go, and that would have to do.

The next afternoon she was still puzzling over Slade's odd reaction to the idea of visiting Three-Stars when she looked up and saw him heading toward the house with a bagful of lemons.

"A peace offering," he said as he handed it to her. "I know I was curt with you yesterday."

Dani smiled and gestured toward the lemons. "So you brought along a tart reminder?"

He grinned. "Something like that. How are the cupcakes coming for Saturday's garage sale?"

"Baked and iced and in the freezer. Two dozen of them. We had to make them today since we'll be so busy tomorrow."

"Am I too late to help with the lemonade?"

"Absolutely not," she said, getting several pitchers out of the cupboard.

When she handed him an old-fashioned hand juicer, he simply stared. "Where's the fancy electric one?"

"I'm sure you can handle this one," she assured him. "It's simple and effective. Life did go on quite nicely before all the modern conveniences were invented." She handed him a knife. "Go for it."

He studied the pile of lemons, the glass juicer and the knife as if they were alien objects. Dani hid a grin at his fierce look of concentration as he began to squeeze the juice from the first lemon. He stared hard at the minuscule amount that wound up in the tray, then looked up at her.

"It's going to be a long afternoon, isn't it?"

She chuckled. "But I promise great rewards for your efforts."

His gaze clashed with hers and held. He rose slowly. "I can only think of one reward that will be worth all this work."

Dani got the distinct impression from that glint in his eye that he was not referring to a pitcher of homemade lemonade.

"And I don't think I'm willing to wait for it," he added, stepping closer.

Before she realized fully what he intended, he lowered his head and grazed her lips with a tender kiss. Dani blinked and stared into Slade's deep blue eyes. He looked a little dazed, but as quickly as that reaction registered in her brain, his bafflement changed to desire and his mouth recaptured hers.

Tenderness rapidly gave way to something far more tempestuous. Dani's pulse quickened, then raced as his arms slid around her waist. Their bodies fit together as perfectly, as intimately as if they'd been carved for mating.

Wild, unexpected sensations rampaged through her, stealing breath and rational thought. All that mattered was that deep, memorable kiss, the skim of flesh against flesh, the taunting rub of fabric over sensitized nipples, the stunning press of masculine arousal.

And the heat. Oh, my, the incomparable heat. Dani thought she had never experienced anything quite like it. She felt it everywhere, warm and liquid where their tongues met, blazing over her skin where his caresses lingered, and raging like a wildfire in her veins.

The kiss lasted forever...and not nearly long enough. When they finally broke apart, both of them breathless and shaken, Dani was speechless. So, it seemed, was Slade. In fact, he looked as if he'd been poleaxed.

She was surprised to see that his hands shook as

he turned away and deliberately reached for another lemon. Surely this wasn't half as shocking to him as it had been to her, she thought as she sank back onto a chair and clutched the edge of the table for some sort of link to reality. Surely he'd experienced a zillion kisses just as devastating.

That dazed look in his eyes, however, said otherwise. And it was enough—more than enough, in fact—to give Dani the courage to move on with her plan to capture Slade Watkins's heart and his boys for her own.

Chapter Five

"And there were horses and cows and real live cowboys," Kevin told Slade exuberantly over supper the next night. "Jake Dawson used to ride bulls in the rodeo. He was a champion. Sara even rode on a bucking bronco in a contest." His eyes were wide with the wonder of it all. "I want to grow up and live on a ranch just like Three-Stars."

Slade winced. His son could have done exactly that had Slade made peace with Kevin and Timmy's grandfather. He tried to imagine what his son would think of him if he knew Slade had walked away from such an opportunity, if he guessed that his father had shunned the very life-style that had so entranced Kevin on their outing with Dani to her family's ranch. This was precisely the outcome he had feared when she had first suggested the visit.

Slade glanced at Timmy, who was curiously silent. "What about you? Did you have a good time?"

"It was okay, I guess," Timmy said.

The lack of enthusiasm was such a contrast to Kevin's delight, so at odds with Timmy's usual exuberance, that Slade was instantly on the alert. Something had clearly happened to his older son on that visit to the ranch.

"Did you go for a horseback ride?" he asked, trying to tread carefully on tender young male pride as he sought answers.

"Yeah."

"It was awesome," Kevin chimed in. "I rode this palomino pony named Buttercup. It's a sissy name, but she was a great horse."

"And you, Timmy?"

The question was greeted by absolute silence, until Kevin finally ventured, "Timmy fell off his horse."

Timmy's face contorted with anger. "You weren't supposed to tell," he shouted at Kevin as he shoved back his chair and ran from the room.

Guilty tears welled up in Kevin's eyes. "I promised I wouldn't tell," he admitted to Slade, "but he didn't have to go and get all crazy. He didn't get hurt or anything. It's not like you're going to say we can never go again, right?" Worry creased his brow. "You won't, will you?"

"Of course not," Slade said at once. "But I'd better go talk to him. Finish your dinner, okay?"

Kevin stood up, too. ''Maybe I'd better go and tell him I'm sorry,'' he said stoically.

Slade scooped up his youngest and hugged him. For all of the boyish squabbling in which he and Timmy engaged, they were fiercely loyal. Of the two, Kevin was by far the most compassionate. Guilt radiated from every pore over hurting his much-idolized big brother's feelings.

''You can apologize later,'' Slade told him. ''Let me see him alone for a bit. I'll bet I can get him back in here in time for dessert.''

Kevin's expression brightened. ''Is it one of Dani's pies?''

''The rest of the apple pie,'' Slade confirmed. ''Now eat your vegetables.''

Kevin's eyes narrowed. ''Will Timmy have to eat his, too?''

''Yes, Timmy will have to eat his, too, if he wants dessert.''

With Kevin grudgingly forcing down the cooked peas and carrots, Slade took his time climbing the stairs. He could just imagine Timmy's humiliation at having fallen from the horse in front of Dani. His pride would be in tatters.

With the injury to Timmy's ego so fresh, Slade doubted anything he could say at this point would make a difference, but he had to find some way to convince Timmy that falling from a horse wasn't the end of the world. He had to do a far better job than his own father had done at explaining that not everyone was suited for ranch life.

He knocked softly on Timmy's bedroom door. He could hear muffled sobs inside. Doubting that Timmy would willingly admit him, Slade opened the door, crossed the room and stood over the huddled figure of his boy.

"You okay?"

"I'm going to kill the squirt," Timmy managed to choke out between sobs.

Slade held back a smile, then sat on the edge of the bed. Timmy instinctively scooted closer without looking up at him.

"I don't think killing him will be necessary," Slade told him. "Kevin feels really bad that he tattled on you, but he was right to do it this one time, you know."

Timmy lifted his tear-streaked face and stared with openmouthed astonishment. "You said tattling on people is practically a sin."

"Sometimes, when you care a lot about someone and you can't help them, you need to let someone who can help know what's going on."

"It was just a fall off a stupid horse," Timmy countered. "It's not like I broke my arm or committed a crime or something."

"Was Dani there when you fell?" Slade asked, trying to get to the heart of his son's dismay.

His son bobbed his head once as his cheeks flushed with embarrassment.

"That must have felt pretty awful," Slade suggested, aching for his son and recalling all too vividly his own humiliation under similar circumstances.

Timmy nodded again.

"Did you get back on?"

Timmy's chin quivered as he shook his head. "I couldn't, Dad. I just couldn't. I ran away. Dani had to come and find me. She told me I shouldn't feel bad, but I did. I felt dumb. We weren't even out of the paddock or anything. Even Kevin stayed on, and he's just a baby."

"I'll bet Dani has fallen her share of times. And I know her sister Sara did when she was trying to learn to ride a bronco. It's just part of learning to ride."

Timmy sniffed. "That's what Dani said."

"Didn't you believe her?"

"I figured she was just trying to make me feel better. She does that all the time. She jokes around until you forget whatever happened to make you feel bad."

"Dani's pretty terrific, isn't she?"

Timmy's expression began to clear. His eyes brightened. "She's the best." He regarded Slade slyly. "I think she likes you, too."

Slade swallowed hard as memories of that bone-melting, sizzling kiss came roaring back. "What makes you think that?" he asked in a choked voice. That kiss had been a warning to steer clear of her, unless he wanted to risk both of them getting hurt eventually. Passion didn't equal love. It never had. One could exist quite nicely without the other, as-

suming love between men and women even existed
at all.

Now, love between parent and child, that was
something else again, he thought, gazing at his son.
Given his background, he'd been stunned by the
strength of that bond. Timmy and Kevin might baf-
fle him most of the time, dismay him quite a lot of
the time and infuriate him some of the time, but the
strongest emotion he felt through all of it was love.

From the first moment he'd held them in his arms,
his heart had been lost. He'd vowed then and there
that they would always know exactly how much
they meant to him, that he would never try to control
and dominate and, failing that, then dismiss as his
father had.

"I think she likes you because of the way she
looks at you when you come around," Timmy told
him, his expression thoughtful as he struggled to put
his conviction into words.

"How does she look at me?" Slade asked, unable
to curb his curiosity.

"All mushy like they do in the movies right before they kiss." He studied Slade intently. "Have
you kissed her yet?"

"If I have, it's none of your business," Slade said
stiffly.

Timmy's expression turned all too knowing.
"You have, I'll bet. What's it like kissing a girl?"

"You'll find that out for yourself soon enough,"
Slade told him. He grinned. "And it's a little like

riding a horse. Sometimes you get it wrong, but it gets better and better the more you do it.''

Timmy's fascination with kissing clearly faded at the mention of horseback riding. His face clouded with concern again. "Did you ever fall off a horse?" he asked hesitantly.

Ah, there it was, Slade thought, the question he'd been hoping to avoid. "Quite a lot, actually. I was younger than Kevin.''

"You rode a horse when you were that little?" Timmy asked incredulously. "How come?''

"My father insisted on it.''

"Grandfather rode horses?''

"All the time.''

"Why?''

Slade was sure that given enough time he could come up with an evasive answer that would have satisfied Timmy and kept him away from a subject he would rather avoid. After his conversation with Dani, though, he wondered if he'd be able to steer clear of it forever. Maybe it was time to bite the bullet and admit a few things about his past, about his sons' heritage.

"Because he's a rancher," he said eventually.

Timmy's eyes widened predictably. "Like Mr. Wilde?''

"Exactly like Mr. Wilde," he said with an edge of dry humor his son couldn't possibly understand.

"How come you've never told us that before?''

"Because your grandfather and I don't get along so well, so I don't like to talk about him much.''

"He's still alive?" Timmy asked, disbelief written all over his face. "I figured he was dead."

"No, Duke Watkins is very much alive."

"Where does he live?"

"In Texas."

"Can we go there sometime?" he pleaded, clearly oblivious to Slade's distaste for the subject. "Not to ride horses or anything," he added hurriedly. "Just to see our grandfather."

"I don't know about that," Slade said evasively.

For once Timmy didn't argue. He apparently had too many questions.

"Do we have a grandmother, too?" he asked.

Slade nodded.

"Wow, awesome!" He hesitated. "Do you think they'd like me and Kevin?"

Slade sighed, then said candidly, "They would adore you."

"Wow! Wait until I tell Kevin."

Before Slade could stop him, Timmy rushed from the room and clattered down the stairs, shouting for his brother. So much for old secrets, he thought with a sigh. His past was about to come out of the closet with a vengeance.

He hoped like hell Dani would be satisfied at the can of worms she'd opened up by dragging the boys out to the ranch. Of course, he had a feeling that even if she'd known precisely what the outcome would be, she would have gone ahead with her plans anyway.

But when the boys started clamoring for a trip to

Texas, maybe he'd just send Dani along with them so she could get a firsthand look at what a real control freak looked like. Maybe then she'd come to appreciate her own father's far more mild-mannered form of meddling.

As distraught as Timmy had been the night before over embarrassing himself in front of Dani, Slade decided he had no choice but to go with the boys on Saturday when they planned to hold the yard sale at Dani's. When he saw relief wash over Timmy's face he was glad he'd reached that decision. Apparently a little fatherly moral support was just what he needed to face Dani again.

They arrived precisely as planned at seven o'clock. The yard sale had been advertised around town on handmade posters, with a scheduled start time of eight. Already, though, Dani looked besieged. Half a dozen cars were parked at the curb, the occupants looking like an anxious swarm of locusts.

The Bleecker boys were struggling to get their card table opened and ready for the lemonade sale. Two identical twin boys, Dirk and Kirk Hinson, their mouths covered with chocolate frosting, looked as if they'd already eaten up most of the potential profits from the cupcake sale. Only that daylong trip to Three-Stars had probably saved them from being eaten straight out of the oven two days ago.

"Thank goodness you're here," Dani said, pausing long enough to hug both boys. The look she exchanged with Slade was so frazzled, so unexpectedly vulnerable that he concluded right then he would have fought dragons for her.

"Did this get just the teensiest bit out of hand?" he inquired, very glad he'd insisted they leave Pirate at home that morning. The dog would have been the last straw. Dani might very well have flipped out right before his eyes with Pirate chasing everyone in sight.

"Don't gloat," she warned. "Just start carting those boxes in the garage out to the lawn. And if one single person gets out of a car, belt them."

"Is that how you've held them at bay up until now?"

"I waved my shotgun at the first car. Word spread," she told him with a grin.

"I can imagine. I doubt I'll have any trouble with them."

"Oh, you'd be surprised what the sight of a few boxes of cast-off belongings will do to otherwise rational people. I ought to know. I nearly trampled a woman to get that old-fashioned cookie cutter I have in the kitchen. Paid top dollar for it, too."

Slade chuckled at her triumphant expression. "Nothing stands in your way when you want something, does it?"

"Nothing," she confirmed, then grinned at him. "You might want to remember that."

He was still trying to puzzle out the meaning of her remark as she dashed across the lawn to nab the card table just before it upended with three pitchers of lemonade.

"Dad," Timmy prodded. "Dani said to get the stuff in the garage."

"Oh, right," he said distractedly.

"Now," Timmy said emphatically.

"Okay, okay." He followed his son to the garage, where a dozen or more cartons were crammed with every conceivable kind of junk. He couldn't imagine that the combined worth was more than a few dollars. Obviously the avid people in their cars thought otherwise.

For the next half hour he carried boxes and helped to arrange the items they contained on old blankets and tablecloths that had been spread over the grass until it looked like some sort of country patchwork quilt.

At precisely eight o'clock Dani surveyed everything, gave a little nod of satisfaction and gestured toward the growing crowd of would-be buyers. They emerged from their cars like racers exiting a starting gate.

In no time at all the boys were overwhelmed with enthusiastic shoppers. Dani's hair, which she'd tucked into some sort of a knot on top of her head, was coming loose, tendril by silky tendril. Slade had the most incredible desire to sweep a few curls away from the back of her neck and kiss her on that exposed bare skin.

She turned just then and, as if she'd guessed his thoughts, blushed prettily. Then almost at once she returned her attention to a customer who was bargaining enthusiastically for some china knickknack that couldn't have been worth more than a dollar new, but appeared to be selling for $12.50 now that it had a little wear and tear on it.

Slade decided at that moment, with his sons shouting happily over each sale, with Dani clearly in her element and desire slamming through him like a freight train, that he would forever think of garage sales in an entirely different way. Maybe they could have one every weekend. Surely there was enough stuff crammed into his grandparents' attic to keep this crowd going for weeks on end.

"You seem to be enjoying yourself," Sara Dawson, Dani's sister, said, surprising him. He hadn't even known she'd arrived. He recognized her from an occasional glimpse he'd caught of her in town.

"Actually, I'm a little out of my element," he confessed.

"Didn't look that way to me. I saw the way you were staring at Dani. I recognized the look."

He swallowed hard and forced a casual note into his voice. "Oh, and what look would that be?"

"A hunter about to claim his prey."

He chuckled at the comparison. "I expected something a little more romantic."

"Hunger is hunger," she said. "No matter which kind it is." She eyed him intently. "Just where do things stand between you and my sister?"

The blunt question didn't surprise him. The

Wildes were obviously a very direct clan. "Isn't that between your sister and me?"

"Not if you intend to hurt her," she said fiercely. "Then it becomes a matter for all of the Wildes and the Dawsons and the Fords."

"In other words, the Wilde sisters and their mates stick together."

"You bet. And Daddy's the toughest one of us all."

"I'll remember that."

"See that you do." She grinned then. "In the meantime, you might try to knock her socks off. She deserves to have her world go topsy-turvy for once, instead of being the rock who holds the rest of us together."

Slade nodded soberly. "I'll remember that, too."

Dani dashed up just then and scowled at Sara. "What are you telling him?" she said, clearly fearing the worst from her very direct, red-haired sister.

"Not a thing," Sara swore, casting a thoroughly innocent look at her sister.

"You're not meddling?" Dani asked doubtfully.

"Wouldn't dream of it," Sara insisted. "That's Daddy's job."

Dani faced Slade. "Is she telling the truth?"

He exchanged a grin with Sara, who was looking a little worried suddenly about where his loyalties might lie. He decided, for the sake of family peace and his own peace of mind, he'd better stick to her story just this once. "Absolutely," he swore.

"Good," Dani said, obviously relieved. She held

out her hand to him. "Come with me. I need help with Mr. Garrett. He's trying to steal my favorite old records for practically nothing. I told him I had to check with someone who'd submitted a sealed bid that was higher than what he was offering."

Slade grinned at the blatant lie. "You love this, don't you?"

"What's not to love? I get rid of all my junk. People leave with treasures they're sure they got at bargain prices."

"Bargain prices, my eye. I saw you negotiating over that silly china dog. You bamboozled that woman."

"Did not. She would have paid twice that. She has a collection. She knew exactly what she was getting. So did I."

"If you say so. Just remind me to watch my back if we're ever trying to strike a deal."

She reached up and patted his cheek. "Don't worry. I'll always give you fair warning before I bamboozle you."

Again there was a spark in her eyes that struck him as downright dangerous. He couldn't for the life of him figure out what was behind it.

Before he could worry too much about it, he was caught up in the negotiations for a bunch of dusty old 78 RPM records that were probably collector's items. The old man he was supposedly bidding against had an avaricious gleam in his eyes that suggested there was a lot more room for bargaining.

Just as Slade figured they had reached top dollar,

a flustered, gray-haired lady wearing a loose-fitting jogging suit and bright red sneakers jumped off a motorcycle, ran up, listened for the latest bids, then topped them both by twenty bucks.

"Sold!" Dani said before either Slade or the other bidder could react. She threw her arms around the woman. "Congratulations, Mrs. Fawcett!"

"I was so worried we wouldn't get here in time," the older woman said. "Your father was dillydallying all the way over here. He said this whole sale was a bunch of nonsense. He seems to think if you need money, you ought to be coming to him, not selling off your belongings on the front lawn."

"This isn't about the money," Dani protested. "Oh, for goodness' sakes, what's wrong with him?"

Slade turned and stared at the man in question, who was just now climbing off the Harley and sauntering their way. If he hadn't seen it with his own eyes, he wouldn't have believed it. Trent Wilde wearing a motorcycle helmet and careening around town on a motorcycle with his lady love was about as unexpected as watching sweet little Dani bargaining like Donald Trump.

"Did you get here in time to get those silly records?" he asked Matilda Fawcett.

"No thanks to you," she shot back, drawing grins from Slade and Dani.

"What the devil are you planning to do with them, anyway?" Trent demanded.

"I was planning on inviting you over to dance to

them, but at the moment I wouldn't let you get that close, you old sourpuss.''

Slade chuckled aloud, then tried to hide it as Trent shot him a baleful look.

''Women!'' the old man muttered, and stalked off toward the house.

Dani leaned down and whispered something that had Mrs. Fawcett grinning. After she'd gone off to finish her argument with Trent, Slade asked Dani what she'd said.

''I told her to give him hell.''

''I don't think there's a doubt in the world that she'll do just that,'' he said, laughing at the prospect.

Dani laughed with him. ''The thought of Daddy being one-upped at his own game does hold tremendous appeal, doesn't it?''

''Amen to that,'' Sara said, joining them.

She held up some sort of kitchen doodad that Slade didn't recognize.

''How much for this?'' she asked.

''Be prepared to sell your soul,'' Slade told her with a wink, then went off to check on his sons.

He found them hovering over a cash box overflowing with dollar bills and change. ''Have you ever seen so much money in all your life?'' Kevin asked, clearly awed by their success.

''Remember now, only some of that is yours,'' Slade reminded them.

''But it's still lots and lots,'' Timmy said. ''More than we've ever gotten in our allowance.''

''And more than you're likely to get. I think it

would be a good idea if we opened a savings account with it first thing Monday morning.''

Both boys stared at him as if he'd threatened to banish them to their rooms for a year. "You want us to put it in the bank?"

"It's the safest place."

"But we wanted to buy stuff," Timmy protested.

"Such as?"

"Books," Kevin said, sounding more dutiful than enthused.

"And computer games," Timmy added. "Some that aren't yours."

"And ice cream," Kevin chimed in, finally back in character.

Slade looked into their hopeful faces and decided on a compromise. "You may each buy one book and you can get one computer game together," he said.

Despite the offer, disappointment clouded their faces. "What about the ice cream?" Kevin demanded.

He grinned. "I'll buy that."

The two boys slapped hands in a high five, then Timmy asked, "Can Dani come, too?"

"Of course," Slade said, trying very hard not to reveal that that was exactly what he'd hoped they'd ask. An invitation from his sons would keep him from having to show the woman just how badly he wanted to spend time with her.

According to his logic, if he didn't have to admit to this growing yearning, then it simply didn't exist.

He could go on thinking that Dani Wilde was just a nice woman who was generously filling a huge void in his sons' lives. It was a delusion he intended to cling to as long as humanly possible.

Chapter Six

The outing to the ice cream parlor that Slade proposed grew rapidly from a foursome to a crowd. First Sara overheard the boys inviting Dani and decided to tag along. Then her father and Mrs. Fawcett claimed to have a craving for hot fudge sundaes.

Someone—Dani figured she would never know for sure who—called Ashley and Dillon, who wandered in just as they were taking over the entire middle row of tables. Slade looked a little bemused at being suddenly surrounded by her family.

"This wasn't exactly what you had in mind, was it?" Dani asked, deeply regretting the lack of privacy herself. "Unfortunately, impromptu family gatherings happen a lot with the Wildes. Don't panic at all these interlopers. Daddy will pick up the check."

Slade frowned. "No, he won't," he said adamantly. "This was my idea."

"You'll have to fight him for it, then. He considers it his God-given right as patriarch of the clan. Dillon and Jake have finally stopped arguing."

Slade appeared undaunted. "Then they're not half as sneaky as I am," he told her, grinning. "I gave my credit card to the waitress when we came in the door. Even as we speak the charge is being written up in my name."

Dani chuckled at his sweet innocence. Obviously he didn't understand the ways of small towns yet. "Do you honestly think that any waitress in this town will go against Daddy's wishes?" she asked. "They all know his habits. That credit card will come back to you with an apologetic shrug and without a charge slip attached."

"Care to make a wager on that?" he taunted.

"Sure," Dani said without hesitation. "What are the stakes?"

"You choose."

The first part was easy enough and suited her own devious purposes rather nicely. "Okay, if you win, I'll make you and the boys dinner for a week," she said.

Slade grinned. "Done. And if you win?"

She hesitated over that one, then finally said, "You come to Three-Stars with us next time we go."

His face promptly clouded over. She could see a

storm brewing in his eyes and expected a negative answer, even before he said, "I don't think so."

"You said I got to choose," she reminded him, even as she tried to gauge exactly how painful the thought of such a visit was to him and why. She played her trump card. "I doubt if I'll be able to get Timmy back there without you."

He sighed, his innate sense of parental responsibility obviously kicking in. "You don't play fair."

"Just looking out for your boys," she retorted. "And you."

His eyebrows rose a fraction. "Me?"

"People should always confront the things they fear most."

The suggestion clearly stung. Slade went perfectly still, and his gaze hardened. "What makes you think I'm afraid of Three-Stars?"

"Your reaction when I asked you to go there. What's with you and ranches? It can't be Three-Stars itself. As far as I know, you've never set foot on the place. So it must have something to do with your past."

His stony reaction told her she'd hit the nail on the head. That subtle confirmation was enough to satisfy her for now. She didn't have to know every detail of his antipathy toward ranches. That could come later. For now, she met his gaze evenly. "So," she said gently, "will you come? For Timmy's sake?"

"I'll come," he said tersely, then added, "if you win the bet."

* * *

Slade cursed the day he'd ever gotten mixed up with Dani Wilde and her pushy family. He stopped his car at the wrought-iron gate to Three-Stars and sucked in a deep breath. No matter how often he told himself that this wasn't his father's ranch and that there was no reason on earth to react as if it were, his insides twisted into a knot anyway.

Damn that stupid bet he'd made with Dani. He should have realized she knew her father through and through. Slade never had figured out how Trent Wilde had managed to pay the bill at the ice cream parlor without getting caught at it. Sure enough, though, Slade's credit card had come back with an apologetic shrug, just as Dani had predicted.

As a result, instead of getting a solid week's worth of decent meals, here he was facing his demons. The only thing holding him together at all was the fact that Timmy was clearly more terrified than he was to make the trip down that long, winding driveway.

"I'm not getting on a horse again," he said fiercely from the back seat.

"You don't have to," Slade reassured him.

"But it's so much fun," Kevin argued. "You won't fall this time. You have to try it."

"Dad, make him stop bugging me."

"Kevin, leave your brother alone. It's his decision." Slade glanced into the rearview mirror. "Dani did suggest a picnic by the creek, though. She says we'll have to take the horses to get there."

Timmy looked suspicious. "Why can't we drive?"

"There's no road," Slade told him.

Timmy's forehead creased with a frown as he weighed his options. "I could stay at the house with Sara," he said resignedly, proving just how greatly his fear had been magnified during the past week.

Kevin stared at him with shock. "You'd miss the picnic?"

"Who cares about an old picnic?" Timmy retorted stoically.

"You don't have to decide right this second," Slade told him. "Let's see how you feel when we get up to the house."

"I won't change my mind," Timmy vowed.

"Bet you will," Kevin taunted.

The next thing Slade knew the two of them were wrestling in the back seat, taunts and fists flying.

"Enough," he said sharply, then added a threat that suited his own purposes all too well. "Or no one will be going anywhere. I'll turn around right this second and go back home."

To his deep regret, not even Timmy was willing to risk that, apparently. Uttering a heavy, put-upon sigh, he settled back into the seat as far from his brother as he could get. Kevin glared at him.

The tension lasted until they reached the ranch house. Kevin bolted eagerly from the car, while Timmy trailed along behind, looking dejected. Slade put an arm around his shoulders.

"How about riding with me?" he suggested casually.

Timmy stared at him doubtfully. "On the same horse?"

"Sure. You can sit right in front of me in the saddle."

Timmy considered the new option carefully, then brightened. "I guess that would be okay."

"You won't fall," Slade promised him. "I'll see to it."

Though Timmy was rapidly reaching the age where he shunned public displays of affection, he threw his arms around Slade's waist. "Thanks, Dad."

"You bet. Now go with your brother and pick out the best horse for us, preferably not one named Diablo," he added dryly.

"How come?"

"Just take my word for it. Diablos usually come by their name naturally. They are not gentle creatures."

"Oh," Timmy said. "I'll find us a really tame horse, Dad."

"I'd appreciate that."

As soon as Timmy had run off, Slade paused and absorbed the once-familiar sensations of being on a ranch. The scents of dust and recently mowed grass, the distant lowing of cows, the feel of unrelenting sun on his shoulders, burning even through his shirt. Oddly enough, it wasn't nearly as awful as he'd expected.

"How does it feel?" Dani asked softly, coming up beside him.

"Familiar," he said at once.

"Scary?"

He smiled down at her. "No, this place isn't scary at all." He wanted to add that it was because she was there, but feared that would be far too revealing of feelings he wasn't ready to acknowledge.

"You grew up on a ranch, didn't you?"

He nodded.

"Did you hate it?"

Slade considered the question thoughtfully. "I don't think I hated the ranch nearly as much as I hated the man who ran it. He turned it into a torment." He glanced around at the stark, rugged terrain that was so different from his home in Texas and yet in so many ways the same. "How could any place this beautiful be despised?"

"Like you said, it's not the place. It's the people. Neither Ashley nor I were cut out to be ranchers. Sara got all of those genes. Even so, I didn't leave because I hated my home or the life-style we had here. I left Three-Stars because my father was overbearing and controlling. Now that I have my independence, I actually enjoy coming back." She grinned. "Once in a while, anyway."

"Meaning, I wouldn't mind going home again either, now that I know who I am?" he asked.

"Something like that."

He gazed into her huge brown eyes. "How did you get to be so wise?"

"I'm not wise, just practical. It takes a lot more energy to fight the past than it does to accept it."

"I told Timmy about his grandparents the other day."

Surprise and pleasure lit her eyes. "Did you, now? I'd say that's progress."

"Of course, now he and Kevin are clamoring to go to Texas for a visit," he said.

"Will you take them?"

"I was thinking I'd let you do it."

She chuckled. "Oh, no, you don't. You deal with your father. I've got trouble enough with my own."

Before they could debate whose parent was worse, Kevin and Timmy came running up.

"When are we going on the picnic?" Kevin asked. "My tummy's empty."

"After that huge breakfast you ate this morning?" Slade asked skeptically. "That was just over an hour ago."

"I'm a kid," Kevin reminded him. "I need lots and lots of energy."

"You just heard that I baked chocolate chip cookies, didn't you?" Dani said. "Sara blabbed."

"She said you fixed a whole feast," Timmy confirmed. "Fried chicken and coleslaw and potato salad." He gazed at Kevin. "And what else?"

"Biscuits, I think. And iced tea."

"That's a lot of work for food that will be gobbled up in a nanosecond," Slade observed.

Dani shrugged. "It's a pleasure to cook for

healthy appetites for a change. It's no fun to fix big meals for one person.''

The comment was innocuous enough that Slade couldn't imagine why it set off warning bells. He looked deep into Dani's eyes, searching for some sort of ulterior motive, some hint that she was using her excellent cooking to weave an ever-tighter web around them all. Surely every woman had been taught that the way to a man's heart was through his stomach. In the case of the Watkins family, where edible meals were few and far between, that slogan had the ring of truth. Would Dani Wilde exploit such a thing?

She returned his gaze, though, with a perfectly bland expression. "I'll just run up to the house and get the picnic basket," she said. "Boys, ask Jake to help you saddle the horses."

Kevin's eyes widened. "Really? We get to saddle them ourselves?"

"With Jake's help," she reminded them as they ran back toward the paddock.

Slade debated following them or going to assist Dani. He suddenly wanted desperately to put some distance between them. Every time he was around her lately, he realized that he was more and more drawn to her in ways that went beyond a physical yearning.

She was so sweetly generous, so direct and honest that he was beginning to let down his guard around her and that, he reminded himself sternly, would be a huge mistake.

Women were all alike in some ways. They wouldn't be satisfied until they got their hooks into a man. But then they changed, just as Amanda had, practically from the day they'd exchanged vows. He wouldn't risk going through that kind of transformation again. It would be hard on him. It would be devastating to the boys.

Gazing into Dani's soft, expectant eyes, however, he had trouble imagining her ever turning devious and cunning, especially since those were traits she hated so in her father. His wariness gradually faded away.

"Come on," he said, taking her arm. "I'll help you with the basket, before the boys keel over from hunger."

"Do you really think that's likely?" she teased.

"No, but they think it is. They'll pester the daylights out of us until they're fed. We'll be eating this picnic long before noon. I guarantee it."

A few minutes later, as they returned to the paddock with the food, Dani asked, "How did you convince Timmy to get back on a horse, by the way?"

"It was mostly the promise of your food," he admitted. "That and my agreeing to let him ride with me."

She brightened, clearly approving his ingenious solution. "You know something, Slade Watkins? You are an absolutely wonderful father."

Dani's assessment washed over him, warming him more than she could ever imagine. Despite all of the worry-filled nights he'd spent, despite all of the doubts he'd ever had about his parenting skills, especially since he'd been flying solo, he suddenly felt reassured. This woman, who had such a natural gift with children, thought he was a decent father. He wanted desperately to believe that.

Amanda had been far stingier with her praise. In fact, she had accused him on more than one occasion of being a distant, uninterested parent. Looking back, he could see how she had come to that conclusion, though.

In an effort to keep peace with her, he had often avoided family outings. He'd felt the boys were better off without his presence, if that meant they wouldn't be subjected to the tension that existed between him and their mother.

After Amanda's death he had spent weeks consumed by guilt. The boys had learned to avoid him and his dark moods. The sad truth was he couldn't think of the last time he had spent as much carefree, happy time with Timmy and Kevin as he had since they'd moved to Riverton and been taken under Dani Wilde's wing.

"Thank you for saying that," he said, then added wryly, "There are a lot of people in Riverton who would disagree with you, though."

"Oh, really? I haven't heard anyone complaining about the boys lately, have you?"

"No, but that's your doing more than mine. You're the one who's been keeping them out of mischief."

A smile spread across her face. "Then I'd say we make a perfect team."

Impulsively, Slade bent down and brushed a quick kiss across the tip of her upturned nose. Naturally, the casual contact had the expected consequences. Desire rocketed through him. If two eager little boys hadn't been waiting for them, if a bevy of interested observers hadn't been within a few yards of them, he might have followed through on the invitation that promptly sprang to life in her eyes.

Even as that awareness came to him, he realized that he was falling ever more deeply under Dani Wilde's spell. And that terrified him more than the prospect of half a dozen futile, argumentative encounters with Duke Watkins ever had.

Dani thought things with Slade were progressing rather nicely. Every now and again, she thought she caught a hint of puzzlement in his eyes and once in a while there were signs of outright panic, but in general he seemed content enough with their growing friendship.

The boys, of course, were playing straight into her hands. She already loved them as much as if they were her own. The time she spent with them fulfilled her in ways she had only imagined.

Listening to them chatter excitedly, to the pounding of their footsteps through the house, even to their bickering filled her with incomparable contentment. Could anything be more satisfying than nurturing children and watching their individual personalities blossom?

Not that the relationship was all one-sided. Kevin and Timmy were clearly benefiting from her influence. They were less and less troublesome with every day that passed. Even Myrtle Kellogg had commented on it. They seemed to thrive on her attention and her laughter, to say nothing of the nutritious food she was fixing for them. They hadn't pleaded for a bologna sandwich and potato chips in a week now. And Timmy had finally overcome his fear of horses, thanks to her and Slade. The picnic had been a rousing success.

The boys were also discovering what it meant to have discipline and a regular schedule. Set boundaries reassured a child. Goodness knows, her own father had made his rules and expectations clear enough. She hadn't noticed that she and her sisters had suffered as a result of it, even when they'd fought hardest to break free. In fact, that battle, too, had made them stronger.

All in all, her theories about child rearing were being borne out rather well. She was relieved to know she hadn't just imagined what a good mother she could be.

The only flaw came every day at five or five-thirty, when Timmy and Kevin left for home with their father. Her heart ached as they walked away. It was growing increasingly difficult not to gather them close and beg them to stay. All of them, Slade included.

On rare occasions she was forced to admit that at first he had been almost an afterthought, a means to an end. He had the ready-made family she craved.

Now, though, she was more and more drawn to his wry sense of humor, his obvious love for his sons, his surprisingly easy blending with her own rambunctious family.

Moreover, she loved the fact that he wasn't intimidated one whit by her father. If she had ever made a list of the things she was looking for in a mate, that would probably have topped it. Sara and Ashley had succeeded in finding strong men who could hold their own against Trent Wilde. She wanted the same for herself.

And then, of course, there was the fact that Slade's kisses absolutely, positively made her toes curl. With every second that she spent around him, this unfamiliar craving was building, demanding that the spin of her senses be carried to the only logical conclusion.

In time, she reminded herself. First things first. She had to find just a tiny niche in Slade's heart, so that when she made her outrageous suggestion that they make their relationship permanent, he wouldn't simply stare at her in shocked silence.

She wasn't sure that she could bear it if he laughed in her face, either. She had to be sure, or at least as sure as a woman could ever be, that he would consider her idea thoughtfully and examine it on its merits alone.

His boys needed a mother, there was little doubt

about that. The only question remaining, and one for which she didn't have a convincing answer yet, was whether Slade Watkins realized just how badly he needed a wife.

Chapter Seven

Dani was leading a small parade toward the general store when she ran into Matilda Fawcett. The retired teacher beamed at her.

"I see you found yourself some helpers," she said, referring to Timmy and Kevin, who were each pulling a wagon filled with baked goods. "Never hurts to have a couple of strong young men around when there's work to be done."

Timmy and Kevin puffed up with pride at being referred to as young men. Dani suggested they take the pies and cookies on to the store, while she chatted with the teacher. They were only too eager to comply, since they'd been promised a dollar each to spend for helping her. It would probably take them an hour at least to decide what they wanted to buy with their money. She'd discovered they were astonishingly frugal.

When they'd gone, she asked, "How have you been, Mrs. Fawcett?"

"Plucky as a spring chicken," she retorted. "That father of yours has an amazing way of keeping life interesting."

"I can imagine," Dani said.

In fact, she found the whole idea of her father courting a woman to be a rather intriguing concept. He and her mother had sometimes seemed to be a single unit, their thoughts and actions blending so perfectly, so smoothly that it had given all three of their daughters a probably misguided notion of the possibilities of marriage. There seemed to be a good many more fireworks going on in Sara's marriage to Jake and Ashley's to Dillon. Matilda Fawcett seemed likely to bring that same sort of spark into her father's life.

"It seems to me that you're every bit as good for him as he is for you," she added, thinking of the battles she'd already witnessed between her father and her former teacher. "You don't take any of his nonsense."

"Heavens, girl, I've been around far too long to let anybody run my life," the older woman announced. "I live as I see fit. If he can't accept that, well, he'll just have to go sniffing around in somebody else's garden."

Dani was sure that that threat alone was more than enough to keep her father in line. He would take it as a challenge to stay in Matilda Fawcett's good graces.

"Well, believe me, you have my blessing. I haven't seen my father so happy in a long time. I'm sure Ashley and Sara feel the same way."

Mrs. Fawcett's expression brightened. "Why, thank you. Hearing you say that means a lot. I must say you've been looking awfully content yourself lately. Mothering becomes you."

She lowered her voice to a conspiratorial whisper, though no one was nearby to hear. "Any chance you'll be making it permanent? I'm sure the whole town would give you a medal if you'd keep those two mischief-makers in hand."

Dani was fairly certain that the question was being asked on her father's behalf, rather than out of concern for the town's well-being. Apparently not even the independent-minded Mrs. Fawcett was above a little meddling for the sake of a man she cared about.

"We're just taking things day by day," she said blithely, refusing to add to any speculation that might be going on around town or, more precisely, in her father's head. "Slade and I have a relatively informal arrangement regarding my caring for the boys."

Mrs. Fawcett grinned at the diplomatic answer. "And what sort of arrangement have you made for caring for him?" she inquired.

Dani gaped, then tried to recover. "Mrs. Fawcett—"

She never got to finish the sentence. Mrs. Fawcett cut her off. "Oh, stop with that Mrs. Fawcett and that stuffy tone," she chided. "It's a natural enough question, given the way you two look at each other. Even if your father hadn't been going on and on about the two of you, I would have noticed it myself the other day. Neither one of you paid a bit of attention to your ice cream or to the rest of us, for that matter. You were too caught up in each other. Your father mentioned it, too."

Dani nearly groaned aloud. "Please, tell me you're kidding. I really don't need him getting any more ideas than he already has on the subject of Slade and me."

"Then you'd better put some distance between you and that young man, because when you're in the same room, only a blind man would miss the fireworks."

"Maybe you and Daddy should go on a vacation," Dani suggested as an alternative. "A very long cruise to Alaska would be lovely this time of year."

Mrs. Fawcett chuckled. "If you think even I could convince your daddy to leave town with you on the brink of a big romance, then you don't know him half as well as you think you do."

"Couldn't you at least try?" Dani asked wistfully.

"I don't think so," she said apologetically. "If the truth be told, I'm getting a kick out of watching the two of you myself."

"I'm so pleased I can provide the family with some entertainment," Dani retorted sourly. If they were this enthralled with the slow mating dance she and Slade were performing, she could just imagine how tickled they'd be if they discovered she had every intention of asking the man to marry her.

It took Dani several more weeks to convince herself that her plan to claim the Watkins family as her own wasn't half as outrageous as she'd first thought. With every day that passed, her courage and determination were building. She intended to have her family by the end of summer, come hell or high water.

As she spent more and more time with Timmy and Kevin it was clear that they were desperate for a mother's touch and gentle guidance. Now, though, their bids for her attention were more in keeping with typical boyish antics, rather than destructive misadventures. Her neighbor hadn't uttered a complaint about the noise or trampled flowers in nearly a week now. In fact, Dani had noticed her outside on several occasions chatting with the boys while her favorite soaps blared unnoticed in the background.

As for Slade himself, even after all their afternoon chats and occasional outings with the boys, she didn't exactly know what to make of him. In some ways he was the quietest, most self-contained man she'd ever met. Compared to her father's rowdy ways, Slade's sometimes brooding demeanor made him seem downright aloof and mysterious.

It was the undercurrent of vulnerability, which surfaced from time to time, that actually tugged at her heart. He was as much at sea with his sons as she would have been in the high-tech computer world that he inhabited.

But that, too, was changing. Slade and the boys were bonding more each day. Slade was taking more and more time from his work schedule for impromptu visits to Dani's. He'd even agreed to help coach a summer league baseball team that Timmy had pleaded to join. Slade had been so stunned and pleased by Timmy's desire to participate in a team sport that he'd even offered to buy the team's uniforms.

All in all, they were beginning to fit in, not only in Riverton, but in Dani's life. She built her days around the arrival of the boys in the morning and the arrival of Slade at day's end. She might have forced herself to be content with that if she hadn't seen the potential for so much more. As it was, her day of reckoning was drawing closer, the day when she'd have to speak up and make her wishes known. Otherwise the boys would be back in school and the need for a full-time baby-sitter would have passed. Her daily contact with Slade and his sons would taper off until she had nothing left.

Sara and Ashley were living proof that taking risks paid off. Dani refused to consider what might happen if she was the one sister whose risk-taking cost her everything.

She glanced toward the dugout across the field, where Slade was surrounded by eager boys and one intrepid girl. It was the bottom of the ninth inning and the team was very close to its first victory. The bases were loaded and the next scheduled batter was Hattie McDonald. Dani could just imagine the debate going on as the boys tried to convince Slade and their other coach that a substitute should be sent in.

She jumped up and began to yell for Hattie. Soon other mothers around her were doing the same. Slade shot a glance her way and grinned. He leaned down, whispered something to the freckle-faced girl and sent her toward the plate.

Kevin stared, wide-eyed. "He's going to let a girl hit?"

"It's her turn at bat," Dani said, defending the decision.

"But she's a *girl*."

"If she was good enough to make the team, then she's good enough to play."

"You liberated females make me sick," Lonny Hinson announced, glaring down at her from the row behind her in the bleachers. "That little brat is going to cost us the game. He should have sent in one of the twins."

Lonny's twin boys had been warming the bench all afternoon because they'd missed the past two practices. Lonny had been seething ever since he'd heard what their punishment would be. He was especially peeved that Hattie was replacing one of them.

"Would you rather win or do what's right?" Dani asked, undaunted by his scowl. "Isn't this supposed to be about kids having fun and learning about following the rules and about team spirit?"

"It's about winning," Lonny declared, just as the smack of the bat making contact with the ball sounded.

Their gazes flew to the field, where the ball was dropping into a huge space between the left fielder and the center fielder. Neither of the boys had been paying much attention. Clearly they'd been convinced that Hattie would never get a ball out of the infield, if she hit it at all. It was a full five seconds before either of them even reacted to the ball coming their way.

As two runs scored on the hit, Dani turned a triumphant expression to the chagrined man behind her. "Any comment?"

Lonny, whom she'd known since high school when he'd been a macho bore as well, was plainly torn. "Okay, so she's got some power," he conceded grudgingly.

"Remember that next time you want to see her plucked from the lineup in favor of a boy who's been skipping practice, even if he happens to be one of yours. Maybe this will be a wake-up call to the guys that they're not indispensable," Dani told him with a grin, then gazed at Kevin, who was obviously dumbfounded. "You remember that, too, sport. Your dad knew what he was doing sending her to the plate."

She and Kevin made their way to the winning side of the field, where a victory celebration was already under way. They arrived just in time to hear Slade announce, "Pizza for everyone."

"Us, too?" Kevin asked his father.

Slade's gaze met Dani's. "Of course, you, too. If you'd like to come."

Dani couldn't imagine any place on earth she'd rather be, not even when the noise level in the pizza shop reached deafening decibels. Or when twenty filthy little children used grungy hands to reach for slices of pizza, which they stuffed into their mouths with little regard for the manners she was sure they'd been taught. She watched and listened, finally sighing contentedly.

"You love this, don't you?" Slade asked, leaning in close enough to be heard. His stubbled cheek, which lent him a surprisingly sexy air, grazed hers, sending goose bumps chasing down her spine.

She grinned at him. "I do. Does that make me insane?"

"Not in my book, though I have to wonder why you didn't decide to become a teacher. With your patience and your ingenuity, you'd be fantastic."

She couldn't bring herself to tell him that she'd balked at studying education because she'd always anticipated having a home of her own, children of her own who would need her full-time attention. She had not been one of those women who had a conflict over the desire for family and a career. She'd never wanted to have it all, as the saying went. To her a family *was* everything.

She took in the chaos around her. This was what she'd wanted, every noisy, messy, exuberant moment of it.

She looked straight into Slade's blue eyes and caught what she thought was a flash of desire. Today, she decided right then. Today was the day she was going to ask Slade Watkins to marry her, though she thought something a little more private than their current circumstances was called for.

"Will you stop by the house later?" she asked, her breath catching in her throat as she waited for his reply.

"Actually, the boys are supposed to spend the night with the Bleecker kids," he said, clearly leaving it to her whether to withdraw the invitation or to let it stand, sending an entirely different message.

She met his gaze evenly, drew on every last ounce of courage she possessed and declared boldly, "All the better."

Then there was no mistaking the flash-fire of desire in his eyes. Unexpectedly, he reached over and curved a hand around the nape of her neck and brushed a kiss across her lips.

"Is that a yes?" she asked, between hoots of laughter from the boys who'd caught the gesture.

Pointedly ignoring them, Slade asked, "Is seven too early?"

"Seven is just perfect."

Just perfect, she thought contentedly, her vivid imagination already in overdrive. It was going to be a night neither of them would ever forget.

Seven! Why on earth had she ever said seven would be perfect? It was six forty-five and her hair was soaking wet, her best blouse needed ironing and the skirt she'd decided at the last second to wear had a pinned-up hem she'd been meaning to stitch up for a month.

Maybe, if the gods were with her, Slade would be late just this once. Not likely, she thought with a sigh of resignation. The man had a built-in clock. If he said he would be over at seven, then he wouldn't be so much as ten seconds past that.

Which meant settling for a pale pink blouse, rather than the hot pink one she'd hoped to wear, and for white linen slacks instead of the skirt. She used the fifteen minutes to try to blow-dry some style into her hair. She was actually satisfied with the results by the time the doorbell rang, precisely at seven.

Slade had used his time to clean up, as well, proving that she hadn't imagined that he recognized the evening as the momentous occasion she envisioned. His hair was still damp from a recent shower. He'd shaved off that sexy stubble. He was wearing chinos and a soft blue dress shirt, the sleeves rolled up, the collar open. She concluded there was something far more enticing about a man who'd taken steps to dress down a formal shirt than there was about one wearing a sports shirt. Maybe it was because he looked a little as if he was already on his way to undressing.

"Something smells wonderful," he said at once.

"The pot roast," she suggested.

He grinned and reached out to tuck a stray curl behind her ear. "And here I was thinking it was your perfume."

She blinked at the unexpected compliment and the tender gesture. "You noticed," she said, suddenly shy.

"It reminds me of your garden, the way it smells in the morning with the dew still on it."

She stared into his eyes, trying to see if he was somehow making fun of her, but he seemed serious. She was surprised. She had never once thought of Slade as having a particularly romantic or poetic bone in his body. Not that he wasn't a sexual creature. Goodness knew, the man radiated sex appeal from every pore. But that was different from spouting the kind of sweet remarks that could charm a woman's socks off.

Convinced he was sincere, she smiled. "Thank you."

He grinned. "The pot roast smells wonderful, too, though after all that pizza, I'm not sure I'll be able to do it justice."

Oh, dear, she'd never thought of that. She'd hoped to fill his stomach with good food and then, when he was thoroughly mellow and content, to pop the question.

"Maybe after a glass of wine you'll feel more like eating," she suggested. She certainly needed the additional bravado the wine would impart. She practically raced toward the kitchen, where she'd left an open bottle of her best Bordeaux to breathe, beside two of her best crystal wineglasses.

"I hope you like red wine," she said, tilting it so quickly that it splashed all over the counter.

Slade quietly removed the bottle from her shaking hand and set it back down. He touched a finger to her chin and forced her to meet his gaze.

"What's wrong? Why are you so nervous?"

"I've never done anything like this before," she blurted, then realized he couldn't possibly have any idea what she was talking about or how momentous she intended the evening to be.

Even so, a knowing gleam lit his eyes. His lips curved into a soft smile. "Then we'll take it one step at a time," he promised, just before he captured her mouth in a kiss that could have melted the entire Alaskan tundra.

For one frozen instant Dani realized that he'd misinterpreted her intentions completely, but then she recognized that it didn't matter. Slade Watkins was going to make love to her, she realized with a belated flash of insight. Someone with more experience could have guessed his intentions right away.

She was going to let him, too. In fact, she was going to encourage the seduction. With the power of passion on her side, a mere proposal was going to be a snap.

Despite her resolution she was tentative as she slid her hands up his chest, then into his still-damp hair. She stood on tiptoe to fit her body more intimately with his, thrilling at the way he was the one who suddenly stilled now. She was both terrified and eager, but it was eagerness that won.

Her inexperienced senses drank in everything, the way his body heated wherever she touched, the intoxicating, masculine scent of his aftershave, the sound of his breathing growing ragged as their kisses deepened and pulled them toward an inevitable mating that had been in the cards since the day they'd met.

"Your room?" Slade queried eventually, his eyes dazed with desire.

More than ready to discover everything, all the secrets of passion, she said, "Upstairs, first door on the right."

As if she were the featherlight heroine of a movie, he scooped her up and cradled her against his chest as he climbed the stairs, whispering kisses across her forehead and cheeks as he went.

Dani had never felt such a wild stirring of sensations. No one had ever made her feel so much like a woman. Her virginal insecurities and doubts fled replaced by a woman's confidence. In fact, confidence soared with each caress she dared and each touch that Slade returned.

Her body shivered as he gingerly stripped away

the clothes she had debated so long about before choosing. When she was wearing nothing but a bra and panties, feeling more exposed than she ever had in an equally revealing bathing suit, he stood back and studied her as intently as any artist had ever considered a model before putting brush to canvas.

Eventually, he dragged his gaze back to clash with hers. "You are so beautiful," he murmured. "So incredibly beautiful."

Surprisingly, she felt beautiful at that moment. Ashley had always been the declared beauty in the family. Her successful modeling career had only confirmed what the family had always known. Sara and Dani had taken a back seat to her.

And, yet, at this instant, Dani was certain that no woman could possibly feel as deliriously desirable as she felt.

Slade, in the heat of passion, was a revelation. As distracted as he might be in his day-to-day life, as distant as he could sometimes be, he was neither of those things now. His attention was riveted on her, and Dani blossomed under his increasingly deliberate caresses, the sure strokes of his hand across breast or thigh, the teasing, tormenting brush of his fingers across the most intimate of places.

She was enthralled with everything, but most of all with the man who was so thoroughly dedicated to pleasuring her. She could sense his own restraint in the bunching of his muscles, in the occasional tightening of his jaw or a quick, tormented moan. And yet he never lost his concentration on her needs.

That intensity didn't surprise her half as much as the expression of genuine pleasure that accompanied each shocked reaction she uttered, each tiny signal that she gave that her body was slowly, inevitably surrendering to him. He seemed to revel in his ability to ignite this new and wondrous fire inside her.

When, at long last, he poised above her, she was trembling with need and a raw hunger to make this final, most sensuous discovery.

"Please," she whispered. "Now."

"Yes, now," he replied softly.

He entered her slowly, with only a brief moment of startling pain, then withdrew just as deliberately. His mouth closed over her breast, sending shock waves crashing over her. Each sensation created its own magic. And then they blended into something so compelling, so incredibly powerful that Dani thought she would die from the wonder of it.

Again and again he repeated the pattern until she was crying out with frustration and urgency. Her hips thrust up, seeking him, drawing him in, until finally there were no more games, no more sweet torment, only the riotous pleasure of an explosive climax that rocked them both to their very cores. The purest joy she had ever felt cascaded through her and settled in her heart. She had waited—far too long, she had sometimes thought—but it had been worth it. Nothing could have equaled this. Nothing.

"Oh, my," Dani murmured as she sank back against the mattress.

Slade's body—his incredible, heart-stopping

body—remained tangled intimately with hers. When he would have lifted himself away, she held him close.

She'd learned something in the past hour, something totally unexpected. Not just her dream was wrapped up in this man, but her heart.

The stakes of the game had just escalated wildly, but Dani refused to let that daunt her. With her hands framing Slade's face, she looked straight into his eyes.

"Marry me," she said with the quiet serenity of a woman who'd found everything she ever wanted and was determined to have it.

Before he could hide his stunned reaction, before he could utter a word, she kissed him, deeply and thoroughly, just to prove that the suggestion wasn't half as outrageous as he might think.

When his expression remained dazed, when it appeared he was about to murmur some sort of polite, instinctive response that would have dismissed any such notion forever, she touched a finger to his lips.

"Don't answer me yet. Think about it."

If she had her way, it was unlikely he'd be able to think about anything else for some time to come.

Chapter Eight

Slade was absolutely certain he couldn't have heard Dani correctly. He thought she'd asked him to marry her. Was it possible that out of the blue, just like that, the woman had proposed?

Of course not. Women didn't do that sort of thing. He shook his head to clear it, but the same words echoed and then he remembered belatedly that it was one of the infamous Wilde sisters with whom he was dealing. They were notorious for doing the unexpected.

"Marry me."

There it was again. No matter how absurd it seemed, it sure as hell sounded like a marriage proposal. He couldn't think of any other spin to put on two words as direct as those.

Not that they weren't in the sort of intimate situation at the moment that might stir thoughts of marriage and a future in some women. Hadn't he warned himself of the potential for that very thing with Dani? Hadn't he reminded himself again and again that she was a forever kind of woman? She'd been a virgin, which should have been proof enough that she didn't take sex lightly.

But even knowing all of the potential dangers in terms of emotional entanglement, he hadn't been able to resist her. In fact, the past hour had been incredible, as tempestuous as any he'd ever spent. Dani had been everything a man could ever want in a lover—sweetly sensual, wildly passionate, generously giving. A lover, though, not a wife.

The thought of marrying again had never crossed his mind. Marriage was a sore subject with him. If he had his way, he would never chance it. His marriage to Amanda had been a terrible mistake, one he didn't plan to repeat. Surely he had made that clear to the woman beside him. Even if he'd never said the words, he'd dropped clues, danced around the subject, done everything, in fact, except spell it out.

Apparently he hadn't been clear enough, he realized as he gazed into expectant brown eyes. The subject had deserved explicit statements, not innuendos.

Shock left him speechless for several minutes. Embarrassment rendered him tongue-tied.

He thought about the past few weeks. Had all the signs been there? Had he missed the fact that she was falling for him? He'd been convinced that she was far crazier about the boys than she was about him.

Oh, sure, the sparks of desire had been in her eyes every now and again. Otherwise, they wouldn't have found themselves in the middle of her bed on a hot and humid July night. He certainly couldn't blame their presence here on Dani alone, either. She'd flat-out admitted to him earlier that she had never done anything like this before, and the evidence had been there, too. She'd been a virgin and eager enough to change that.

He cursed his insensitivity. He had taken advantage of a sweet, innocent virgin with nothing more on his mind than the night ahead. She'd clearly had more on her mind. A lot more.

But marriage? How the hell had he missed that one coming?

Now that it was out in the open, though, he was thunderstruck. Feeling a little shaky and a lot desperate, he reached for his pants and then his shirt. He needed clothes—and neutral turf—for the difficult conversation they definitely needed to have right this second, before things got any further out of hand.

"Maybe we'd better talk about this somewhere else," he suggested.

"Someplace less...cozy?" she inquired, looking amused and not the least bit offended by his less-than-enthusiastic response to her proposal.

"Exactly," he said, dragging on his shirt and

heading for the door, impressed in spite of himself with her calm. Any other woman would have been totally humiliated by his stunned reaction. Dani appeared to be taking it in stride.

"Fine," she said.

She was still so blasted cheerful he wanted to spit. In fact, he concluded after daring a look straight into her eyes, she seemed to have expected his reaction. That suggested that this wasn't some impulsive, spur-of-the-moment idea that he could dismiss with an appropriate dose of logic. He had the distinct impression she was going to have a laundry list of positives to counter anything he could come up with in his befuddled state of mind.

"Dani—" he began, but she waved him off.

"It's okay. You go ahead," she insisted. "You can serve up that pot roast if you're hungry now. I'll be downstairs in a second."

As eager as he was to be gone so he could collect his thoughts, Slade had the feeling that he ought to be staying right where he was. Who knew what other crazy ideas she might come up with when he wasn't looking. Still, he went.

Guilt and dismay warred inside him as he paced up and down in the kitchen and waited for the uncomfortable conversation that was ahead. He had to find some way to let her down easily, to explain that although he appreciated so many things about her, he wasn't in love with her. He didn't even believe in love anymore.

Maybe telling her that would be enough. A romantic like Dani would be shocked, maybe even appalled by such a declaration. She probably wouldn't even want a cynic like him in her life.

Or she might consider him more of a challenge than ever, he concluded wearily. She was that kind of woman. She was a Wilde.

As he paced and debated, he tried to ignore the aroma of that damned pot roast, but its allure was almost as powerful as that of the woman who was awaiting his reply to her proposal. He couldn't recall the last time he'd had a decent pot roast. It was something his mother had enjoyed serving, but Amanda had disliked most meat. The scent of well-cooked beef and spices and rich gravy had his mouth watering and his head filling with memories he was so certain had been forgotten. Memories of home. Memories of a mother who'd been a whole lot like Dani in her ability to nurture, if not in her ability to stand up to the stubbornness of Duke Watkins.

In what felt a lot like an act of rebellion—though he couldn't for the life of him determine against whom—he finally scooped some meat and vegetables onto two plates and irritably slammed them onto the table.

Dani breezed in a minute later, wrapped in some sort of slinky, sexy robe that was practically indecent. He couldn't seem to drag his gaze away from the way it clung to her breasts, outlining her nipples in provocative detail. Where the devil were the jeans and T-shirts she usually wore, he thought to himself. She'd lingered long enough upstairs to put on real clothes. He'd expected protective barriers, layers of them, in fact. Instead, she'd sashayed down here looking all tousled and wanton. She was practically irresistible.

Determined not to succumb to this latest temptation, he sat down and focused his attention on forking the pot roast into his mouth, bite by deliberate bite. When he finally dared to glance up, he saw that she was watching him with that same amused, knowing expression.

"It's okay, you know. You don't have to worry about giving me an answer now," she reminded him. "I know my proposal must have come as something of a surprise, but it makes sense, really."

Surprise? That was an understatement, if ever he'd heard one. Slade stared, trying to follow her unspoken logic. When he couldn't, he echoed, "Makes sense? How?"

While his head was still reeling, she systematically piled reason upon reason, until the whole idiotic scheme did begin to make a crazy sort of sense. There were sensible, practical reasons that seemed to have a lot to do with her being able to fix meals and get them on the table. The pot roast seemed to be her primary exhibit. Hearing that, he dropped his fork so quickly that gravy splattered on the pristine tablecloth.

Then there were emotional considerations, such as how much she adored the boys and vice versa. He had no arguments for that, none at all.

Finally she added what she clearly considered the coup de grace.

"Also, it's clear to everyone in town that the boys were..." She hesitated. "Well, they were a bit out of control, if you don't mind my saying so."

Slade minded her saying so like crazy, but truth was truth. Until Dani had taken charge, Timmy and Kevin had seldom missed an opportunity to stir up trouble. At ten and eight, there was only so much damage they could cause. He had hated to think what they might do when they hit their teens.

Even so, it rankled to have this woman remind him he had been a lousy father until she had prodded him into doing otherwise. He had been doing the best he could—under trying circumstances—to make up for past neglect.

In fact, he had convinced himself that he and the boys were starting to do just fine on their own. And while Kevin and Timmy were definitely more of a handful than he'd expected, he thought things were going rather well. Nobody had gotten poisoned from his cooking or broken any bones so far.

Of course, he was forced to admit that Dani might have been largely responsible for that. She'd been sending more and more meals home with the kids lately, and she was responsible for them for a good percentage of their waking hours. She'd even sided with Timmy and somehow convinced him to coach a baseball team, even though it was a sport he'd never played himself. Thanks to Dani, they were turning into the damned Brady Bunch.

But even if he was satisfied with the way things had been going, he gathered that others in Riverton weren't as impressed with his parenting skills. In fact, memories of the boys' first pranks died hard. The disapproving glances he continued to receive every time the boys misbehaved were beginning to get on his nerves. Dani had a point about that.

"They're a little rambunctious," he conceded. "But they've been much better lately."

She gave him that same sneaky, knowing smile. "Since they've been spending time with me?" she suggested.

Slade swallowed hard. He'd always believed in giving credit where credit was due, but he sensed that this time an admission was going to be a tactical blunder. Still, he couldn't bring himself to deny her claim.

"You have been a good influence, no doubt about it." He eyed her warily. "Maybe we could work out some sort of ongoing business deal even after the summer ends. They'll be back in school soon. I'd pay you to look out for them after school, you know, to do the things a mother would do, like bake cookies and stuff."

"Should I fill in for you at parent-teacher conferences, too?" she inquired a little tartly.

Slade winced. It was the first little slip in her composure, but he couldn't take much pleasure in it. In fact, as soon as the words had come out of his mouth, he had recognized exactly how insulting they were. She was proposing to marry him. He was offering to pay her to be a surrogate mommy, when she clearly wanted to be the real thing.

He fully expected to feel one of those fantastic blueberry pies of hers smashed in his face. Surprisingly, the prospect wasn't all that distasteful. He'd grown very fond of those pies. And, if he were being totally honest, of the woman who baked them.

Instead of being smothered in blueberries, though, he heard a distinctly merry chuckle that had a disconcerting effect on his pulse. When he met Dani's gaze, he saw that far from taking serious offense at his suggestion, she found it—or his continued resistance—thoroughly amusing. Clearly, Dani Wilde was a most remarkable woman.

He took another look at her. Less than an hour ago they had been as close as it was possible for two people to be, and yet now it was as if he were seeing her for the first time.

He took the time he should have taken earlier to survey her closely. He started with the brunette hair she wore in a style that curled softly around her face, moved down past the decidedly feminine curves barely concealed by that slinky robe and ended with the tips of her bare toes. The flame-red nails, usually hidden inside dusty cowboy boots or sneakers, were so incongruous with her sweet image that the sight of them alone was enough to stir his blood.

He had the feeling that he had unleashed something in bed, something that was dangerous and wild, both in himself and in her. Even sitting here in the middle of her kitchen, with a plateful of tempting pot roast, his favorite food, all he could think about was carrying her back upstairs and tossing her onto that soft mattress and making love to her again.

And again.

But if the first time had drawn a proposal, what would happen following a repeat? Would she have the preacher waiting downstairs? He wouldn't put it past her, given her attachment to surprises.

That determined, optimistic gleam in her eyes was definitely disconcerting. The lovely, gentle woman with the flyaway brown hair struck him as someone dedicated to a mission, and he seemed to be at the center of it. Her absolute serenity in the face of all his doubts and skepticism was the most disconcerting thing of all.

His gaze rose to clash with hers. Only one word came to mind, and it was at the heart of everything.

"Why?" he asked.

She smiled in a way that suggested aeons of feminine secrets, then shrugged. "Because the three of you need me," she said simply.

Did they? he wondered. Certainly the boys needed someone to guide them and love them, to give them the kind of tenderness he wasn't sure he understood. He, however, needed no one except his sons. He wanted Dani, but that was something else entirely.

Suddenly, before he could try to explain the difference to her, Slade gazed into her eyes and saw the kind of yearning that could break a man's heart.

He guessed, then, that the real need here was hers, not theirs. Or perhaps some blending of the two.

How had he missed it? Her father's attitude, the meddling of her sisters, all of it pointed to an almost desperate desire to see Dani wed and settled down with a family of her own.

He suspected it was more than the fact that she was almost thirty and unwed. It was the fact that she was a woman who had always craved a home and family. Nurturing was what she did, as naturally and enthusiastically as another woman might climb a corporate ladder. So far, though, she'd been lavishing all that love and attention on her father and sisters and on friends and neighbors.

She was impatient with the pace of her own love life, and now literally everyone in town seemed dedicated to seeing that she got her heart's desire. He wondered how many of them viewed him as her last and best hope.

She certainly seemed to see herself as a woman who'd run out of options. And maybe in Riverton she had. The town wasn't exactly crawling with bachelors. With the exception of a few old codgers on outlying ranches, who would no doubt have been glad to have a comely companion and decent cook around.

But Slade could have told Dani about a whole world that craved the kind of rich and unconditional love she had to give. There seemed little point in wasting it on a man as uninterested in love and marital ties as he was. He'd played that game and failed at it miserably. There was no reason to think he could get it right the second time around. In the end, he would only disappoint her.

"I'm not asking you to love me, if that's what's worrying you," she said bluntly, somehow reading his mind.

"Just to marry you," he said, holding back a desire to smile at her simplistic view of the deal she wanted to strike.

She nodded.

"Why would a beautiful, intelligent woman like you marry without love?"

Her thoughtful expression lasted for some time before she said, "It seems to me there are two kinds of love—that blinding, love-at-first-sight kind and the kind that grows slowly."

She smiled at him and shrugged as if they were discussing something as simple and uncomplicated as growing a vegetable garden, rather than one of life's most intricate and tricky relationships.

"I'd rather take my chances on the latter," she explained. "I'm willing to put in the time and hard work it takes to make a marriage succeed. I won't cut and run when that first glow wears off."

Again Slade was startled by her unknowing insight into his own heart. He'd been wild about Amanda, stunned by her beauty and enchanted by her zest for life. That sweet haze of enchantment had worn off for both of them practically before the ink was dry on the wedding license. When it was gone, there had been nothing left except two little boys who wondered why their mother never came home anymore.

When Amanda had died a slow, painful death from injuries she'd received in another man's car in a middle-of-the-night wreck, Slade had faced the knowing looks and expressions of sympathy with stoic, bitter silence. He hadn't been able to get away from Denver and all the gossip fast enough. The small Victorian home in Riverton, left to him years ago by his maternal grandparents, had been a godsend, a haven to him as a child, remembered warmly as an adult.

Perhaps Dani Wilde was yet another godsend. Impulsively, he leaned over and kissed her, drawn by some indefinable need of his own. It was a soft, tender exploration that brought a sigh to her lips and reassurance to his heart.

Suddenly the whole crazy idea did begin to make sense. Or maybe he'd just succumbed to the desperate longing he heard behind her words. He might not know a thing about women, but he understood a whole lot about desperation. He'd faced it head-on the day he'd awakened and realized that the rearing of his two sons was entirely in his hands.

Because it suited his purposes, he tried to convince himself now that maybe a marriage of convenience wouldn't be half as bad as a marriage based on love that turned sour before the first anniversary.

Because it had felt so good, so right, he kissed her once more, tasting the sweetness of her lips, lingering to savor the softness. This kiss lasted far, far longer. It was clearly a prelude to something. Perhaps the future, perhaps just more of the intoxicating lovemaking that had brought them to this point.

"Was that a yes?" she asked, sounding breathless, her eyes sparkling with excitement.

He brushed his thumb across her lower lip and shook his head. At the quick flaring of disappointment in her eyes, he allowed himself a smile.

"But it was a definite maybe."

Chapter Nine

Maybe. Truthfully, it was more than Dani had had any reason to hope for. Slade hadn't laughed in her face. He hadn't flat-out said no, though he'd looked for one interminable minute as if he might.

He'd said maybe. And if she knew almost nothing else about him, she knew that Slade Watkins always meant what he said. He was a man of few words, but he made each and every one count.

She clung to that knowledge all through the night as she cradled the pillow that still carried his wonderfully intriguing, purely masculine scent. She, Dani Wilde, had actually popped the most important question of her life and Slade Watkins had said maybe. It was enough to keep her downright giddy for a month.

But she didn't have a minute, much less a month to waste. She couldn't sit back now and hope nature took its course.

No, if Slade was going to be considering her marriage proposal, then she was going to have to do everything in her power to weave some sort of spell he wouldn't be able to resist. She would have to keep him so off balance, so fascinated with her that marriage would eventually seem as inevitable to him as it did to her.

The trouble was she'd never been much good with playing provocative games or flirting. The stakes had always seemed too high. She was too self-conscious, too vulnerable to risk being rebuffed. Her brazen marriage proposal to Slade had been her first foray into a more daring pattern for her life, and it had scared her practically spitless.

But she'd survived. She'd faced her fear of rejection and overcome it. Now it was on to step two, whatever the heck that was. She hadn't entirely expected to ever need a step two. She'd been counting on a quick yes or no. Now that she needed a more detailed plan of action, she was at a loss.

Fortunately, she had two sisters who'd never been the least bit shy around men or at a loss about much of anything. Sara had won her husband with that outrageous all-or-nothing bet. Ashley had mistakenly bopped Dillon with a lamp and managed to win his heart anyway. Surely they would be good for some sisterly advice. An easy-to-follow, impossible-to-screw-up list—Five Steps To Catching The Man

Of Your Dreams—would be nice, especially if step
two was an awe-inspiring, spectacular doozy that
would practically eliminate the need for steps three,
four and five. She vowed to speak to them on Sunday.

Of course, getting her two sisters alone during the
traditional Sunday family dinner at Three-Stars was
almost as complicated as the logistics for staging a
military maneuver. Dillon was so disgustingly be-
sotted with his wife that he rarely let her out of his
sight for long. Sara had just discovered a more do-
mestic side to her nature. She tended to fuss over
the dinner preparations, much to the dismay of their
longtime housekeeper, who considered the kitchen
to be her domain. Annie's expression turned increasingly sour each time Sara invaded the kitchen. Ashley and Dani spent an awful lot of time smoothing
ruffled feathers.

And then, of course, there was her father. He
seemed to have some sort of radar when it came to
detecting a scheme afoot. He spent most of Sunday
hovering around Dani, asking questions about Slade,
poking and prodding about their relationship until
she wanted to scream. She vowed then and there to
invite Mrs. Fawcett to dinner next Sunday just to
distract him.

It was Sara who finally rescued her.

"Daddy, why don't you go out to the barn and
check out the new foal?" she suggested. "Jake isn't
happy with the way she's developing."

Jake looked a little startled, but he was smart enough to guess that something was going on and to take the broad hint that the men's presence wasn't needed.

"Come on, Trent." He glanced at his brother-in-law and rolled his eyes. "You, too, Dillon. Ashley will still be here when you get back."

"If he's lucky," Ashley retorted, then kissed Dillon soundly before adding, "And he is always very lucky."

Looking very reluctant, Dillon tore himself away and headed for the barn with the other men. Dani suspected that what he knew about horses would fit on the head of a pin, but he enjoyed Trent's and Jake's company well enough to sacrifice a few minutes with his wife to be with them.

"Okay," Sara said to Dani the minute the men were out of earshot. "What is wrong with you? You've been jumpy as a june bug since you got here."

"It's love," Ashley said, her own gaze still on the doorway through which her husband had disappeared. "I recognize the symptoms."

"Could you forget Dillon for just a minute?" Sara said impatiently. "Dani needs us." She looked at Dani. "You do need us, don't you?"

"Though it pains me greatly to admit it, I do," Dani confirmed. "I need you to tell me how to convince a man that he can't live without me."

They didn't seem especially surprised by the request.

"Slade, I presume," Sara said.

"Who else? Have you seen any other candidates around town?" Ashley commented. "So, where do things stand between the two of you now?"

Dani described exactly what had transpired the night before. Actually, she stuck pretty much to the conversation she and Slade had had. There was no point in telling her sisters that it had followed a seduction that had finally, at long last, ended what she'd been convinced was the longest virginity on record. If they knew about that, they'd chase Slade down with a shotgun and the whole marriage thing would be out of her hands. She wanted him, but on her own terms.

Instead of solid, reliable advice, though, her description of her dilemma drew hoots of laughter. She regarded the pair of them with indignation.

"A fine lot of help you are," she muttered.

"But, Dani, you can't be serious," Sara protested. "You can't mean to just walk up to a man you've barely met and propose."

"That would be so—" Ashley began.

Dani cut her off. She didn't need a lecture. She needed help.

"Weren't either of you listening? I've already done that. It's a fait accompli," she reminded them. "All I want from the two of you is advice on how to get him to accept."

"You've asked Slade Watkins to marry you," Ashley said, her expression incredulous.

"Isn't that what I just said?" Dani snapped impatiently.

"A man you barely know," Ashley said, echoing Sara.

"I've known him for weeks now," Dani protested.

Sara looked equally as dazed as her younger sister. "I don't believe this."

"I have," Dani replied with a defiant lift of her chin. "Now, would you tell me why that's one bit different from anything you two would do under the same circumstances?" She scowled at Sara. "Weren't you the one who suggested I just find some candidate for fatherhood and get pregnant without even bothering with a wedding? Is this any worse than that?"

"But how could you?" Sara asked, ignoring Dani's question. "It sounds so...so desperate."

Tears stung Dani's eyes. They didn't get it. She hadn't expected this kind of reaction from her sisters, of all people. They, more than anyone, knew how important having a family of her own was to her. Turning to Ashley, who had grown quiet, she thought she detected a stirring of sympathy. With a familiar flash of temper, Ashley, too, scowled at Sara.

"And you weren't desperate when you proposed that bull-riding contest to Jake?" she demanded of Sara. "Let's give Dani a break here. Obviously this is important to her." Turning back to Dani, she asked, "What did he say?"

"He said maybe," Dani said, unable to keep just a hint of triumph out of her voice. "I need to turn that into a yes, preferably in a hurry."

Sara looked more dismayed than ever. "You aren't pregnant, are you?"

"Oh, good grief," Dani muttered.

"Well, the question is not that outrageous," Sara said defensively. "You said you wanted to get married in a hurry."

"I'm thirty, for goodness sakes. It's time, if I ever expect to have any babies of my own."

Ashley turned a quizzical expression on Dani. "Do you love him?"

"I don't know exactly what I feel," she admitted, keeping to herself the tingly way she felt in his presence, the warmth that spread through her when she so much as thought of Slade or his boys. Those feelings deepened with each moment she spent in their presence. Was that love? Or just the start of it?

Then, of course, there was the magical way she felt in his arms. For now, though, that was private. It was going to stay that way, if she had anything to say about it. Based on Ashley's and Sara's initial reactions to what she had told them, some secrets were definitely better kept even from a woman's closest confidantes.

"Then why would you do this, if not for love?" Ashley asked reasonably. "I don't get it. Thirty is not that old. You can have babies for ages yet. You can adopt more. You can fill the whole house with babies, if that's what really matters here."

"Whether she'll admit it or not, she wants a husband, too, and she's doing it because she's convinced Slade is her last chance," Sara commented. "I told you she's desperate."

Dani was beginning to regret opening up this entire can of worms. She also bitterly resented being labeled as desperate. She viewed her actions in a far more positive light.

"I'm just going after my dream," she snapped. "Both of you should know all about that. I didn't make fun of you when you fought tooth and nail to get the ranch, Sara."

"No, you didn't laugh. But you sure as heck tried to talk me out of that bronc-riding contest."

"Because you could have been killed," Dani explained for the millionth time. "This is different." She frowned at Ashley. "I supported you when you wanted to run off to New York to become a model."

Ashley sighed. "That's true."

"You say you tried to stop me from being hurt, but you could be hurt, too," Sara protested.

"It's not the same," Dani argued. "The only thing I'm likely to bruise is my pride, and even that won't happen if you two will stop making judgments and just help me."

Whatever her own misgivings, Ashley shot a quelling look at Sara. "I say we do it, right, Sara?"

Though her expression was still as skeptical as ever, Sara nodded slowly. "Well, of course," she said. "I never said I wouldn't help. I just said the whole idea is—"

"Sara!" Ashley and Dani warned together.

Sara grinned. "Okay, okay. Preposterous or not, if you want Slade Watkins, we'll show you how to get him. The man won't know what hit him."

There was something different about Dani. Slade noticed it the minute he strolled into the kitchen where she was dishing up a fresh batch of chocolate chip cookies for his two eager sons.

After what had happened between them Saturday night, Slade hadn't been especially eager to stop by on Monday. In fact, he'd actually dropped the boys off first thing in the morning without so much as tooting the car's horn by way of a friendly greeting.

He'd spent the rest of the day telling himself that he was a cowardly fool. One part of him might be totally terrified of seeing her again, but another part was as anxious as a teenager caught up in the wonder of hormonal overdrive.

He struggled with his conscience—which was screaming loudly for him to get out before somebody got hurt—and his libido, which was demanding he find out if Saturday night had been some sort of lust-driven fluke.

Ignoring her was no solution at all. She was there in his head, anyway, plaguing him with that damned marriage proposal. It was the thought of the probable hurt in those huge brown eyes if he were to suddenly change his daily pattern of visiting that eventually drew him inside.

He hadn't known exactly what sort of reaction to

expect from her. Certainly it had not been her casual, friendly greeting that was no different from the way she'd greeted him on any other occasion. She acted as if she'd never uttered that impetuous, potentially life-altering proposition.

But there was something different about her. He could feel it, but he couldn't put his finger on it. He checked out the obvious—her hairstyle, her makeup, her clothes—and still couldn't account for it. He looked for more subtle changes in mood or attitude, but those eluded him, as well. Obviously he wasn't nearly as perceptive as he'd wanted to credit himself with being.

He perched on a kitchen chair, distractedly accepted the warm cookie she offered, and prepared to conduct a more thorough survey.

"Dad, why are you staring at Dani?" Kevin asked. "Staring's not polite."

It wasn't getting him the answers he wanted, either, Slade decided ruefully. He shot a look at his son and wondered what perversity caused Kevin to recall such admonitions only when he could use them to embarrass his father.

"No, it is not polite," he conceded. "I'm glad you remember that."

"So, why are you?" Kevin persisted.

Slade glanced at Dani and noticed that she, too, seemed fascinated with Kevin's query or, more likely, with his yet-to-be-spoken reply. He could see he wasn't likely to wriggle off the hook on this one.

"Okay, here's the truth," he said. "When I

walked in, it seemed to me there was something different about Dani. I couldn't put my finger on it.''

He deliberately winked at her, throwing her composure into a bit of a tailspin. It was no fair that he was the only one feeling so totally off-kilter here. She blushed prettily.

Satisfied, he added, ''Now, you can't very well compliment a lady without being specific, can you? She'll think you're just trying to flatter her.''

With the color still high in her cheeks, she grinned. ''Let me see if I get this. Compliments are good. Flattery is bad. Is that your code?''

He nodded. ''Pretty much.''

Timmy had taken in the conversation thus far in silence, but now he shook his head in disgust. ''Grown-ups,'' he muttered. He grabbed a fistful of cookies and headed for the back door. ''Come on, Kevin. Let's go play.''

''Can we, Dad? We aren't going to leave right away, are we?''

Slade couldn't have left now if he'd wanted to. He was too intrigued with what had gone on here since he'd left late Saturday night.

''Don't go far,'' he warned the boys. ''And come when I call you.''

''We will,'' Timmy promised. ''Let's go, squirt.''

When the boys were gone, Slade linked his hands behind his head and tilted his chair back on two legs, prepared to do another, even more thorough survey. Dani allowed the scrutiny without comment.

Thoroughly disgruntled that he couldn't put his

finger on the change, he finally demanded, "So, what is it? Your hair?"

"Same as always," she replied, fluffing out the soft, chin-length curls.

"New makeup?"

"Same old blush and lipstick."

"New blouse?"

Amusement danced in her eyes. "Nope. Had it for years."

"You aren't going to help me out here, are you?"

"Afraid not."

Slade gathered that was her last word on the subject. It didn't stop him, though, from spending the rest of the afternoon and most of the evening studying her intently. If his thorough survey disconcerted her in the slightest, she never let on.

Nor did she try to rush him out the door or beg him to stay. She seemed perfectly content to let him make his own choices. In fact, she just went about her merry business, chopping and stirring and tasting some savory-smelling concoction until he was ready to go crazy.

He told himself that it was the aroma of the dinner she was preparing that had him hinting around for an invitation to stay, but the truth was far more complicated than that. He didn't like not being able to figure out the solution to any puzzle. Until he understood what had changed with Dani, it would torment him.

Another couple of hours and a good dinner and he was sure he'd be able to pinpoint the difference.

She looked confident, but then she always did. She looked at home, but this kitchen was her territory. It was where she made culinary magic every day.

He watched her hands as she briskly kneaded dough for biscuits, then cut them out with deft precision and put them into the oven.

"That's a lot of biscuits for just one person," he observed.

She smiled. "I assumed you and the boys were staying. Was I wrong?"

Slade sighed. "We're staying."

"You don't have to look so enthusiastic about it. If you'd rather go home and pop a couple of frozen dinners in the oven, I won't be offended."

"Nothing much offends you, does it?" he inquired, not entirely sure why he found that so blasted annoying.

"Sure," she said at once. "Cruelty, for one thing. Not being thankful for the blessings we've been given. Actually, the list goes on and on."

"You know what I meant."

"Oh, you were referring to the sort of things you do?" she said blithely. "Such as staring."

"For starters."

"I can't imagine any woman who'd mind having you take so much interest in them."

"What about the fact that I haven't so much as mentioned what went on here Saturday night?"

He thought he detected a certain tension in her shoulders, but she faced him squarely.

"Oh?" she said, looking innocent. "Did you

want to dissect it? I'd heard most men preferred not to talk things like that to death."

"And most women do not propose marriage the first time they hop into the sack with a man," he snapped right back. "You are not most women and I am not most men. What the hell is going on with you?"

She ignored his testiness and offered up that same exasperating, knowing smile. "Not a thing," she assured him. "Cross my heart."

"Dani, this isn't natural," Slade protested, feeling thoroughly out of his depth. "You can't just throw an important question like that onto the table and then act as if nothing happened."

"Sure I can," she said blithely. "You said your answer was maybe, and I accepted that. You'll tell me when you've decided one way or the other. Or would you prefer that I nag you to death until you give me a yes or no?"

He stared at her in disbelief. "So until then you'll just let things go on as they were before?"

"Do I have a choice? Will you make your decision any more quickly if I pester you about it?"

"No."

"Well, then, there's no point in my trying, is there?" she asked reasonably.

Slade wanted to grab her by the shoulders and shake her complacent little body until her head rattled. He settled for hauling her into his arms and delivering a bruising kiss that snagged their breath and left them both weak-kneed and trembling. It might not have answered any of the questions he'd been asking, but it did clarify one thing. The attraction that had swept them both away on Saturday was as powerful as ever.

"Oh, my," she murmured, still clinging to his shoulders, her eyes a little dazed.

At least she wasn't looking so damned complacent anymore, he decided with satisfaction.

Unfortunately, the only thing that kiss had done for him was to stir his hormones into a frenzy. He wanted her with a ferocity that scared the daylights out of him. No woman had ever mixed him up so badly. No woman had ever tempted him beyond endurance.

And no woman had ever walked out of his arms and calmly checked on a tray of biscuits as if nothing of consequence had just gone on.

Pride or desperation or just plain desire kicked in and had him reaching for her again. This time the heat in the kitchen had nothing at all to do with the oven and everything to do with the way their bodies melted together to create a steamy union that might have gotten totally, thoroughly out of control had it not been for the thunder of two pairs of sneakers pounding onto the back porch. Slade wasn't quite quick enough to release Dani.

"Oh, jeez," Timmy muttered, skidding to a halt just inside the screen door. "That is absolutely gross."

"What?" Kevin demanded from behind him. "I can't see."

Slade touched a finger to Dani's kiss-swollen lips and smiled. Whatever was different about Dani no longer seemed quite so important. One thing was clearly the same. She wanted him just as desperately as he wanted her.

Unfortunately, at the moment there wasn't a darned thing either one of them could do about it.

"Are you going to kiss her again?" Timmy demanded. "If you are, I'm going back outside."

"Dad kissed Dani?" Kevin whispered. "Wow!"

Wow, indeed, Slade thought, but said only, "You might as well stay. Dinner is almost ready."

"We're staying? All right!" Kevin said enthusiastically.

"Wash your hands," Dani told the boys.

Kevin ran off at once, but to Slade's astonishment, Timmy just glared at her. "You're not our mother. You can't tell us what to do," he practically shouted, then tore back outside. Pirate chased after him, barking furiously.

Dani stared after him, frozen. She looked so hurt that Slade could have paddled his son on the spot.

"Go and find him," she whispered. "He needs you."

"So do you," Slade told her. "What he said was rude and cruel. He didn't really mean it."

"Yes," she said softly. "I think he did. And it's understandable, too. I'm not his mother."

"That's not the point," Slade argued.

"To him it is. Please, Slade. Go talk to him. He's hurting."

Only because he sensed that she would run after Timmy herself and risk more hurt, he left her and went in search of his son. He found him halfway home, plodding along as if he felt totally and completely alone. Pirate was right at his heels, head hanging dejectedly.

Fighting his own annoyance with Timmy's behavior, Slade fell into step beside him and forced himself to try to understand what had brought on his son's outburst.

"You okay?" he asked.

"Do you even care?"

Shocked, Slade just stared at him. "Of course I care. How could you even ask such a thing?"

"Because you're going to ruin everything."

Bemused, Slade tried to figure out what Timmy meant, but it eluded him. "Ruin what?"

"Dani is our friend, Kevin's and mine. You're going to spoil it."

"How am I going to do that?"

"You kissed her, didn't you? Pretty soon she'll get mad at you, just like Mom did, and then she'll go away and never come back."

Tears were streaming down his cheeks as he said it. Slade gathered him close and, for once, Timmy didn't fight him.

Slade was flabbergasted at the workings of his son's mind. If Timmy's pain hadn't been so obvious, if he hadn't believed so clearly what he was saying, Slade would have dismissed it as nothing more than the overly active imagination of a ten-year-old.

How much had Timmy really been aware of when he and Amanda had been fighting? Had he realized how troubled his parents' marriage was? Slade had been so sure that both boys were too young to understand any of the anguish he and Amanda had been going through. Obviously he'd been wrong. On some level, Timmy had been attuned to it.

"You miss your mom, don't you?"

"Sometimes," Timmy admitted. "Do you?"

"Sometimes," Slade said truthfully. He missed the woman she had been when he'd married her, and he was more sorry than he could say that she was dead. She hadn't deserved that.

"Sometimes I get real scared," Timmy admitted.

"Of what?"

"That you'll die."

"I'm not going anywhere," Slade said. "I promise."

A world-weary expression settled on Timmy's face. "You can't promise. Mom didn't mean to get killed, either. What if something happened? Who would we live with?"

Slade cursed himself for not realizing that it was exactly the sort of question that would plague a child in the aftermath of the unexpected loss of a parent. He'd deprived his children of an extended family. No wonder Timmy felt as if he might one day find himself completely alone.

"Would you like to go to Texas so you can meet your grandparents?" he asked impulsively. "Would it help to know that you have more family?"

To his surprise, Timmy didn't seem nearly as eager as he had when he'd first discovered their existence.

"You said you didn't like them."

"I said my father and I didn't always get along."

"Then I'll bet I wouldn't get along with him, either," Timmy declared loyally. "I'd rather live with Dani. I know I told her she wasn't our mom, but I wish she was."

The reply wasn't unexpected, but Slade's heart clenched anyway. The web drawing him and Dani together was getting tighter and tighter. First, though, he had to banish the ghosts from the past that he'd always believed would haunt him forever.

"Will you ask her to keep us?" Timmy asked.

"Not just yet," Slade said. "But you and I will talk about it some more."

"You promise?"

"I promise."

Timmy nodded, apparently satisfied that Slade would keep his word. "Let's go back now. I'm hungry."

Laughing, Slade caught him up in a bear hug. "You're always hungry."

"That's why living with Dani would be so cool. She can cook better than anybody."

Slade grinned. "She sure can."

But it wasn't Dani's cooking that had him hooked. In the past few days he'd discovered that he was well and truly intrigued with just about everything about Dani Wilde. The direct, honest woman who'd proposed to him a few days before was far more complex than he'd ever guessed.

In the lonely dark of night, he found himself wondering if a lifetime of marriage would be long enough to unearth all her secrets. Could he ever stop punishing himself for not loving Amanda enough to try?

Chapter Ten

"Well," Ashley demanded when she dropped in the first thing on Tuesday morning. "Did it work?"

Fortunately Timmy and Kevin were down the street playing with the Bleecker boys. This was not a conversation Dani would have wanted them to overhear. She could feel the color rising in her cheeks, even as a grin spread across her face.

"Yes, it worked," she admitted. "I know I said it was ridiculous to think that some sexy lingerie the man couldn't even see would make a difference, but it did. Slade never took his eyes off me."

She could still feel the warmth of his intense scrutiny, as well as the blistering heat he'd set off with those frustrated, demanding kisses of his. All in all, she considered the experiment a rousing success, even if she had no clue why it had worked so well.

"I still don't get it, though. It wasn't as if I hadn't been wearing lingerie all along," she pointed out.

"You've been wearing underwear," Ashley corrected with a dismissive tone. "Cotton is not sexy, even with little bows and frilly edging. Those skimpy scraps of French lace I bought for you made you feel feminine. Red makes a woman feel practically scandalous. You were unconsciously radiating an aura of sensuality. What do you think all those magazine ads I did were all about?"

Dani supposed it did make a bizarre kind of sense. She'd agreed to experiment with the red, but as for the set of black bra and panties Ashley had provided, she wasn't touching that with a ten-foot pole. If red was scandalous, the black lace was downright decadent. She needed a whole lot more practice at seduction before she put those on.

"Okay, this went rather well," she conceded, "but what do I do for an encore? Strip naked and greet him at the door?"

"An interesting thought," Ashley observed dryly, "but maybe you should wait awhile on that one. It ought to come in handy when the marriage needs a little spark of something. In the meantime, I've brought this."

She opened her huge satchel of a handbag and scooped out a bottle of outrageously expensive French perfume. She'd promoted it for years, so she probably had gallons of the stuff, but Dani was awed by the size of the crystal container nonetheless. A single ounce, a fraction of this size, would have cost as much as she made in a week with her baked goods.

"This ought to do it," Ashley assured Dani. "A little here, a little there and he'll be swooning, or all those print ads I did are making fraudulent claims."

Dani sniffed the slightly mysterious scent with its delicate floral undertones and regarded the bottle skeptically. "Did it work on Dillon?"

Ashley grinned. "Anything works on Dillon. Being married to him is very, very good for my ego."

Dani sighed, fighting off envy. "I'm afraid Slade will provide a much more realistic test of its powers."

"I imagine he will, but I'm convinced this fragrance is up to it." After giving Dani a quick hug, Ashley hefted her weighty bag and headed for the door. "Gotta run. I'm doing a makeover this morning. It's going to be quite a challenge."

"Anyone I know?"

"Matilda Fawcett."

Dani's mouth gaped. "Our retired algebra teacher?"

"Right woman. Wrong spin. We're talking about Daddy's new flame." She paused. "Or his old one, if I understand the infatuation he had for her years ago."

"Do you intend to tell her to scrap the baggy clothes and sneakers?"

Ashley chuckled. "I'm going to burn them and then I am going to turn her into a sophisticated femme fatale. Daddy isn't going to know what hit him."

"About time," Dani said fervently.

"Isn't it just?"

"Whose idea was this?"

"Mine. You have no idea what it took to talk her into it. She seemed to think she was way too old to change."

"How did you persuade her?"

"I told her Daddy needed shaking up. She couldn't argue with me about that. She's promised me a front-row seat tonight when she unveils her new look out at Three-Stars. You should come, too. I know I'm going to enjoy watching his reaction." She grinned. "Almost as much as I'm enjoying watching you trying to land Slade Watkins."

"Watch your step, sister dearest, or I'll do to you what I threatened to do to Sara."

"Which was?"

"Tell Daddy you're about to make him a grandparent."

"Maybe I am," Ashley retorted, hopping aboard Dillon's infamous black motorcycle and revving it up. She looked very, very bad riding that Harley, an effect that clearly delighted her after years of being the town's perfect angel.

She scooted off before Dani could find out whether she was teasing or dead serious. Ashley a mother? What an incredible thought. Dani grinned. That really would set the family on its ear. If anyone had been laying odds on who'd become the first mother, Ashley would have been at the bottom of the list.

The only way Dani could see to beat her to it was to pull off this wedding to Slade in a very big hurry. She studied the bottle of perfume Ashley had left behind. She recalled all the advertisements promising passion and excitement.

"Okay, let's see just how well you live up to all those marketing claims," she muttered. Just in case, she decided she'd better wear the red lingerie one more time.

Dani had followed Ashley's advice regarding the perfume to the letter, and Slade did seem pretty close to swooning. Actually that wasn't quite the right word. He was sneezing his head off. Dani decided she'd either drastically overdone the here-and-there scattering of the perfume or he was just plain allergic to the stuff.

She made a quick trip to the bathroom and washed off as much as she could. When she returned to the front porch he was still sneezing, but that spark of fascination was evident in his eyes. Clearly the red lingerie was a consistent success.

"Are you okay?" she asked, feeling guilty as sin for causing such a dramatic reaction.

"Just a summer cold," he confessed. "It'll be gone in a few days."

Dani couldn't help herself. She chuckled. She had just washed off at least ten dollars' worth of perfume and the man hadn't even gotten the first whiff of it. She looked up to find him regarding her oddly.

"What's so amusing?"

"Nothing," she said. "Just a private joke."

"You have a private joke about summer colds?"

"Nope."

"About me, then?"

She shook her head vehemently at that. "Of course not." She decided she'd better change the subject. Slade might be totally confused at the moment, but he was no fool. If she wasn't careful, he'd add up two and two and figure out what she was up to.

"Do you have plans for this evening?" she asked.

"Not really. Why?"

"I was thinking of taking a ride out to Three-Stars. We wouldn't be long. I just want to be there when Matilda Fawcett shows up."

"Why?"

"You'll see," she said mysteriously. "Want to come?"

"The boys, too?"

"Of course."

His expression sobered suddenly. "Even after last night and what Timmy said to you? I thought maybe you'd be ready to try and put some distance between you and the boys."

Dani sighed. Was he just seizing on that as an excuse to put some distance between all of them? She wouldn't allow that to happen. "I won't lie to you and tell you it didn't hurt, but do my feelings really matter here?''

"Of course they do,'' he insisted before she could finish all she'd intended to say.

"To you, maybe, but it's Timmy I'm concerned about. Did he tell you why he was so upset? I wasn't sure if I should get into it with him today. It seemed better to just let it slide unless he brought it up himself. He hardly looked at me all during dinner last night.''

"Don't blame yourself. He was embarrassed. Ironically, it really had very little to do with you. I'm sure some analyst would say he said what he did because he has unresolved issues about his mother,'' Slade said. "In other words, he misses her and he's scared that I'm going to die, too. On top of that, he thinks I'm about to screw things up and you'll end up leaving us, too.''

"Oh, dear. All that stirred up by seeing one kiss?'' Dani whispered.

"He has a very active imagination. Until last night I had no idea how active. He knew far more than I'd realized how bad things were between his mother and me.''

"You've never mentioned that before,'' Dani said surprised.

"No man wants to admit he's failed at something so important. Someday I'll tell you all about it.''

Slade reached over and brushed a wisp of hair back from her face. "He said something else I think you ought to know, though.''

"What's that?"

"He said if I do die, he wants to come and live with you. Despite what he said before he ran out of here, he thinks you'd make a terrific mom. Did he tell you that?"

There was such a huge lump in Dani's throat she couldn't speak. She shook her head.

"I thought he might. He worried all night long about having hurt your feelings."

"I guessed as much," she said. "He hugged me really hard when he got here this morning. I suppose I didn't really need the words to know what he was thinking."

Slade's gaze caught hers. "Do you need the words to know what I'm thinking?"

She stared into those blue, blue eyes and thought she saw the beginning of something that went deeper than lust, deeper than affection. But even after all she'd done in the past few days, she wasn't quite daring enough to label it love.

"That you can't wait to get to Three-Stars and find out what I'm being so mysterious about?" she teased.

"Hardly. I may be a little curious, but right now that is the last thing on my mind," he assured her. "And if I hadn't caught this ridiculous cold, I'd prove it to you."

Dani regarded him hopefully. "Maybe it's just allergies."

"I don't have allergies."

Maybe he'd never been bombarded by a particular

French scent before, she thought, but kept that possibility to herself. "Too bad. I was thinking that tonight would be the night I'd reveal that difference that had you so perplexed yesterday."

He groaned, then eyed her speculatively. "You're just saying that, aren't you? Because you know I won't risk sharing my germs with you."

"Am I?" she taunted.

"Dani Wilde, you are a tease."

She stared at him, ridiculously pleased by an observation that would have been insulting to many women. "I am, aren't I? How lovely."

"And you're going to drive me to distraction," he observed.

"I am going to try," she promised. And she vowed to herself, she was going to prove to him that he was marriage material.

She leaned down and, oblivious to his cold, kissed him. "Let's get the boys and head for Three-Stars. I don't want to miss the show."

Slade looked perplexed. "What show?"

"Never mind. You'll see soon enough."

A few minutes later Kevin was asking from the back seat, "Why are we going to the ranch at night? We can't ride horses now, can we?"

"Not tonight," Slade agreed.

"Then how come we're going?" Kevin persisted.

"Dani says it's a surprise."

"Oh, wow," Kevin said. "I'll bet it's a new foal. Jake said maybe one day I could have one of my very own. Is that it? Did you buy me my own horse?"

Slade slanted a look at Dani. "See what you've started with your secrets? Maybe you'd better answer that one."

She turned in her seat. "Sorry, sweetie. This isn't about a horse, I'm afraid. It's a grown-up surprise."

Both boys looked puzzled.

"Like somebody's birthday or something?" Timmy asked.

"Not exactly." Dani was regretting making such a big deal of the trip. Neither of the boys was going to be the least bit fascinated by Matilda Fawcett's transformation. She glanced at her watch. "We'd better hurry or we're going to miss the big entrance."

Even though he was clearly thoroughly confused, Slade dutifully accelerated. In another fifteen minutes they were pulling in to the circular driveway in front of the ranch.

Dani glanced around and noticed that Ashley and Dillon's car was there, but there was no sign yet of Mrs. Fawcett. Headlights just making the turn off the highway indicated, though, that she was on her way.

"Inside, guys," Dani said. "I'll bet if you run out to the kitchen, Annie will give you a snack. She almost always bakes sugar cookies on Tuesdays."

"Are they as good as yours?" Kevin asked.

"Who do you think taught me how to bake?"

That was enough to send Timmy and Kevin scampering toward the kitchen just as Sara appeared. She grinned.

"I see you couldn't resist the show, either."

"What show?" Slade demanded again.

"You'll see," Sara promised.

Slade turned to Jake, who was just coming in from the barn. "You've known these two a long time. Do you find them exasperating?"

"That's putting it mildly," Jake said.

"Do you have any idea what they're up to tonight?"

"None. Relax, buddy. It's less painful if you just go with the flow."

"Where's Daddy?" Dani asked.

Sara's grin broadened. "In the living room, innocent as a lamb. He has no idea."

Slade and Jake exchanged a look of pure masculine commiseration.

"Uh-oh," Slade murmured, as they all walked into the living room.

"And here I thought we'd have to wait until the town's Labor Day celebration for any more fireworks," Jake said. "I think maybe I'm going to need a drink for this. What about you, Slade?"

"Definitely."

"Me, too," Dillon chimed in when he heard them. He glanced over at his father-in-law. "And I have the feeling you'd better give Trent a double."

At the mention of his name, her father looked up from the chessboard. "Where'd you two come from?" he asked testily, scowling at Slade and Dani.

"Nobody said you were dropping by. That makes twice in one week. Something must be up." He glanced pointedly at Slade. "You two planning to get hitched?"

Slade swallowed hard. Dani blushed furiously.

"No, sir," Slade responded. "I can't say we've made any plans along that line."

Her father just grunted his disapproval and returned his gaze to the chess game. Ashley appeared to have him in check, which no doubt accounted for his foul temper.

At the sound of the doorbell, all three women went perfectly still. When no one else moved, Jake said resignedly, "I'll get it."

Three pairs of expectant eyes focused first in the direction of the foyer, then on Trent. Dani wanted to be sure she caught her father's reaction at his first glimpse of Mrs. Fawcett. Ashley's pleased expression indicated she thought she'd done a masterful job of transforming the widow.

Quick, light footsteps sounded on the oak floors. Only one pair. Apparently Jake had been struck dumb. Dani figured that was a very good sign.

Just then her father's mouth dropped open and his whole expression lit up. "Well, I'll be," he murmured, rising slowly and crossing the room. It was clear he had eyes for only one person. "Let me look at you."

Dani followed the direction of his gaze and stared. Ashley, indeed, had every right to be smug. Matilda Fawcett might not look like a young girl again, but years had been stripped away. Under Ashley's guidance, her hair had been cut into a becoming bob and had been colored a soft honey blond shade. She was wearing makeup for the first time Dani could ever recall, just a subtle hint of blush, a light sweep of eye shadow and a dab of mascara that emphasized her delicate bone structure and huge eyes.

The sneakers had been traded for high-heeled pumps, and the baggy sweat suits had given way to a stylish suit in pale pink linen with white accents. She had quite a figure for a woman well into her sixties. All that hiking she did around the mountains near Trent's fishing cabin had kept her in fine shape.

"Well, what's everybody staring at?" she inquired with characteristic testiness.

"You, Tillie," Trent told her. "I declare I've never seen you look so beautiful, leastways not since the day I first laid eyes on you back in high school. You were a beauty then and you're a beauty now."

Mrs. Fawcett shot a disbelieving look at Ashley, who gave her a reassuring nod. The teacher lifted her chin then and said, "Why, thank you, Trent. I do believe your eyesight's improved."

The comment drew hoots of laughter and then everyone was complimenting the woman at once. Dani noticed that her father was looking increasingly disgruntled at not being able to get a minute to himself with Mrs. Fawcett.

"You know, Daddy," she began slyly, "since Mrs. Fawcett looks so gorgeous, it's a shame to waste it sitting around out here at the ranch. Maybe you should take her to dinner."

"It's too late for dinner," the older woman said at once. "If we eat at this hour, we'll both be up half the night with indigestion."

"Breakfast then" Dani said, then added impulsively, "in Paris."

That would go a long way toward serving two purposes. Her father and Mrs. Fawcett deserved an outrageous trip. They'd waited a long time—through separate and very happy marriages—before getting this second chance to be together.

It also wouldn't hurt that a trip to Europe would keep her father out of her hair while she tried to land Slade for herself.

Surprisingly, her father took the bait. A wicked, daredevil gleam lit his eyes as he focused all of his attention and all of his charm on the petite woman standing before him. "What about it, Tillie? Should we show these stick-in-the-muds how to live a little?"

"I've always wanted to visit Paris," Mrs. Fawcett said wistfully. She rested a hand on Trent's arm. "I think I would very much enjoy seeing it with you."

"As long as we're going that far, we can't miss Rome," Trent said, already nudging her toward the front door. He cast a deliberate glance over his shoulder before adding, "And the Greek islands would be a great place for a honeymoon."

He had steered the openmouthed teacher out the door before anyone inside could react. If she gave him an answer, they couldn't hear it. Dani was so relieved that her tactic had worked, she had little thought for the implications of this impetuous trip.

"Do you think they'll really do it?" Sara asked, staring after them.

Dani considered the possibilities and laughed. "I think we can count on that much."

"I was talking about getting married."

Dani stared innocently at her sister. "And what did you think I meant?"

"Oh, never mind," Sara said. "Whatever the outcome, I think Ashley deserves a toast."

Dani glanced over and saw that her youngest sister was gazing happily at her husband.

"There's the proof," he told her.

"Proof of what?" Sara asked.

"That Ashley's decision was very smart. A business that helps to build a woman's self-confidence with a little coaching in makeup and style has all sorts of possibilities," he said. "Have you ever seen Mrs. Fawcett look any happier or more self-assured?"

"Sure," Sara retorted. "When she was handing out failing grades in algebra class."

Dillon scowled at her. "Other than that?" He beamed at Ashley. "You've really found the perfect way to make use of your talent and experience."

"You would say that," she teased. "You planted the idea in my head. I just wish I'd taken before-and-after pictures of Mrs. Fawcett. She's a walking advertisement for the business."

"No," Dani corrected. "She is a walking advertisement for the power of love. No offense, sweetie, but the rest is all window dressing."

"Thanks a heap," Ashley said, then grinned. "But I have to admit I'm not the one who put that glow on her cheeks or that sparkle in her eyes."

Not until they were back in the car and the boys had fallen asleep in the back seat did Dani find a moment to ask Slade about his reaction to Mrs. Fawcett's dramatically changed appearance. "What did you think about what happened tonight?"

"I think the three of you are very special," he said approvingly, warmth shining in his eyes. "You gave those two the push they needed to get together. It was a wonderful way to give them your blessing."

"I wonder if Daddy would ever have made a move, if we hadn't?"

Slade laughed at that. "Knowing your father, I'm sure he would have done exactly what he wanted sooner or later. In the meantime, though, he would have driven you all crazy."

"That's true. If we've learned one thing as the daughters of Trent Wilde, it's how to get exactly what we want," she said, then added pointedly, "eventually, anyway."

"In other words, you're masters of your own fates?" he asked thoughtfully.

Dani smiled. "I think you're catching on. I'm just not sure if that's good news or bad."

He winked at her. "Are you trying to suggest that

now that I know, I might as well cave in to the inevitable?''

"I would never be so crass as to make a suggestion like that," she said with feigned indignation. "Just tell me one thing."

"What?"

"Are you weakening?"

"A little," he conceded, amusement glittering in his eyes. "But don't let it go to your head."

"Not a chance," she said. "It's these little challenges that keep life interesting."

Slade reached over and drew her closer, looping one arm around her shoulders as he drove. "Sweetheart, life around you couldn't possibly be anything but downright fascinating."

Dani gave a little sigh of satisfaction, but her pleasure was short-lived. If she was so darned fascinating, then why the devil hadn't the man said yes yet? How could she prove to Slade that the future didn't have to be controlled by the past? The wisest people learned from their mistakes and moved on.

Chapter Eleven

"Dad, I've been thinking a lot since the other night," Timmy said the next morning. He was sitting on the edge of the bathtub watching Slade shave.

"About?"

"I was thinking maybe you and Dani should just get married." He regarded Slade hopefully. "Don't you think that would be a great idea? That way, if you die or something, she'll already be our mom."

Slade practically slit his throat with the razor when Timmy's observation fully registered. He glanced down to find his son staring at him with a sober, thoughtful expression that suggested he really had been giving the matter some consideration. Despite the panic rising in his throat, Slade owed him an equally thoughtful response.

"A few days ago you were worried that I was going to screw things up with her," he reminded him casually, forcing himself to continue shaving, albeit a bit more carefully.

"But you promised you wouldn't," Timmy countered.

"What put the idea of marriage into your head? I thought you were happy with things the way they are, with Dani as your friend."

"Everybody was talking about getting married and stuff last night," he said, proving once again that kids were not above a little eavesdropping. "It sounds like Mr. Wilde is going to marry Mrs. Fawcett, and he's pretty smart. And Sara and Jake and Dillon and Ashley seem pretty happy. I guess marriage can't be so bad, especially if you get to have cake and stuff at the wedding. That's what Annie said. Was she right? Do you have all sorts of great food at a wedding?"

"At the reception, actually."

"So what do you think?"

Slade thought that the pressure to marry Dani Wilde had just escalated way beyond his ability to fight it for much longer. Aside from the opportunity to eat cake, he wondered why Timmy was suddenly so hot for the idea.

"Is there some particular reason why you think Dani and I should be together?"

Timmy considered the question for a long time before saying, "She's real pretty, for one thing."

"True," Slade admitted, thinking of how often

lately she'd plagued his dreams, causing him to awaken with his body aching with desire. "But you don't marry a woman just because she's beautiful."

Timmy remained undaunted. He obviously had a whole list of reasons he was just itching to share.

"She cooks good, better than you, that's for sure."

Slade grinned. "There's no dispute there, but it's still not the reason a man gets married. Besides, we're not exactly starving, are we?"

"Because Dani cooks for us most of the time," Timmy pointed out with some accuracy.

"It's still not the reason a man gets married."

"She's a lot of fun. And she hardly ever yells at me and Kevin. And she likes Pirate. She even lets him come in the house when he's all muddy and stinky. You never do that."

Which meant he and Dani were likely to have their first major disagreement over the damned dog, Slade concluded. That dog was not coming into his house all muddy and stinky, but he kept that to himself for the moment.

"Anything else?" he asked.

"Oh, yeah, and she yells louder than all the other moms at the baseball games."

"Certainly a laudable trait, but I'm not sure it qualifies as a marriage prerequisite."

"Huh?"

"It's not a reason to get married."

"So what is?" Timmy regarded him innocently. "Sex?"

Slade was very glad he'd put the razor down just seconds before that question popped out of his son's mouth. Timmy was ten years old, for heaven's sakes. Was he watching some cable channel Slade didn't know about?

"What do you know about sex?" he asked, frantically trying to formulate an impromptu birds-and-bees conversation in his head. He'd figured he had another year or two before he'd have to get into this.

Clearly oblivious to his father's panic, Timmy said, "My friend Davey Bleecker says it's what grown-ups do all the time."

That was certainly vague enough, Slade thought with some relief. He considered his next question very carefully. Everyone had heard the old joke about the little boy who wanted to know where he came from. After a detailed description of conception and birth, the kid had shrugged and said, "Oh, Jimmy said he came from Peoria."

Fearing he might be in a similar situation, Slade did not want to supply information that wasn't actually being requested, not on this delicate topic. He gazed down at his son. "Was he any more specific than that?"

"Not really. I figured it had something to do with kissing. I saw you kiss Dani the other night, so I figured you must want to marry her."

Heaven protect him from ten-year-old logic. "Kissing is something special that grown-ups share, but it doesn't always lead to marriage." He left the subject of sex out of the explanation altogether.

"How come?"

"It just doesn't, okay?"

Timmy shook his head. "I don't get it." He shot an all-too-knowing look at his father, apparently aware that there was a lot Slade was leaving out. "I'll ask Dani. She's real good at explaining things."

"Forget it," Slade commanded.

"How come?" Timmy asked.

"Just forget it."

He knew in his gut, though, that the instruction might silence Timmy's questions, but his own mind was suddenly working overtime with thoughts of Dani and very hot, very steamy sex. Timmy might not be old enough to understand what went on between men and women, but Slade was.

Suddenly he couldn't wait to see her again... privately. His level of eagerness was so troubling that he perversely resolved to put a little distance between the two of them. They were close enough to the edge of emotional quicksand as it was. Another session of lovemaking and he might as well kiss his independence goodbye.

Slade hadn't shown his face around the house for days and Dani was beginning to worry that all of her plans were about to go up in smoke. She absolutely refused to cross-examine Timmy and Kevin about their father's whereabouts, which meant she had no idea at all what was going on with the man. Maybe he was just lost in cyberspace. She'd heard that kind of thing happened a lot to computer geniuses. She glanced up from the bowl of cake batter she'd been stirring to find Timmy staring at her.

"Everything okay?" she asked.

He nodded.

"How come you're not outside with the rest of the boys?"

"I wanted to talk to you."

She regarded him closely. "Sounds serious."

He nodded. "It's pretty serious."

"Then why don't you pour yourself a glass of milk, grab a cookie and sit down and tell me what's on your mind." She put the batter aside. She'd finish making the cake later. This was clearly more important.

When he sat down without either milk or one of her freshly baked oatmeal raisin cookies, Dani knew the topic was indeed very serious. She pulled out a chair and sat down opposite him.

"What's up?"

"I was wondering about sex," he told her, his blue eyes fixed on her face. "Could you explain it to me?"

If he'd asked her about quantum physics she couldn't have been any more stunned or out of her depth. The question left her absolutely speechless.

"You want me to explain about sex?" she repeated, still not certain she'd understood him correctly, even though the question seemed direct enough. She swallowed hard and tried to buy some time by asking, "What has your father told you?"

"Nothing that made any sense," Timmy said, looking disgusted. "I guess he thinks I'm just a dumb kid or something."

"I'm sure it's not that at all," she told him. She suspected Slade had probably been as dumbfounded as she was.

"Look, I know all about kissing and stuff," he informed her, then added, "but there's more, right? I mean stuff men and women do when they're married?"

Dani nodded, at a loss as to how to get into this. Surely Slade would tell Timmy whatever he wanted him to know, whatever he felt the boy was capable of understanding.

"I really think this is a topic you should be discussing with your father," she said.

"But he doesn't explain," Timmy repeated, his frustration evident. "I told him I was going to ask you."

"Oh, really? And what did he say when you told him that?"

Timmy promptly looked guilty. "He told me not to," he admitted in little more than a whisper. "But I've gotta know, Dani. I've just gotta."

She doubted the urgency was quite as extreme as he was making it out to be. Timmy was ten, for pity's sake. He still thought girls were yucky...with the possible exception of Hattie McDonald, whose batting skill he seemed to admire quite a bit.

"I'll speak to your father," she promised by way of a compromise.

"Couldn't you just tell me?"

"I'm sorry. This should be between you and him."

Timmy looked thoroughly disappointed. "Will you at least tell him to tell me everything this time?" he asked.

His expression was so innocent Dani couldn't imagine that he had any idea what he was asking of her. Still, with those wide blue eyes regarding her so hopefully, she couldn't say no.

"I'll do the best I can to convince him you're ready to hear everything."

A smile stretched clear across his face. "Gee, thanks," he said, bouncing up and grabbing the cookies he'd forsaken before. "Make it soon, okay? It's really, really important."

"The next time I see him. I promise."

It was a few days before she caught so much as a glimpse of Slade, much less got him alone long enough to bring up Timmy's interest in sex.

Cheeks flaming, she decided to be direct. "Timmy wants to know more about sex," she blurted.

Slade groaned. "Damn. I thought I'd settled that with him."

So the topic really was no surprise. His dismay was evident. "Would you mind telling me how the subject came up in the first place?" she asked curiously. "I know he's precocious and all that, but he is only ten."

Slade stared at her for what seemed to be an eternity. Just when Dani was certain he didn't intend to answer, he blurted, "Actually, it started out with a discussion about you and me and marriage."

She blinked at that and murmured, "Oh, my." No wonder he hadn't been coming around lately. She could just imagine how uncomfortable that had made him. It was nice to know, though, that she had Timmy very much in her corner. Even though their relationship seemed on solid enough footing, she'd had her doubts ever since that outburst of his. With kids, you never quite knew what was lurking beneath the surface of their outward appearances.

"Oh my, indeed!" Slade said dryly. "He saw us kissing, assumed that had something to do with wanting sex and was pretty sure that ought to lead to marriage. He's developed an interesting set of moral values at an early age, especially since he doesn't have any idea what he's talking about."

Dani resisted the urge to chuckle. Slade didn't seem to see the humor in it. "Definitely some leaps in logic," she conceded, "but I like the way he thinks."

When Slade started to respond, Dani touched a finger to his mouth to silence him.

"Hush," she said. "I told you before that I'm not in a rush for your decision. Take all the time you want. I know you're not convinced yet that marrying me is a great idea."

"I am about one part," he muttered, though he didn't look one bit happy about it.

"Which part would that be?"

Instead of answering, he unexpectedly hauled her into his arms and crushed her mouth beneath his.

Maybe absence did make the heart grow fonder, after all, she concluded, giving herself up to the desperation in that kiss. She could feel the barely leashed desire slamming through him, even as a matching need rocketed through her. He was hard, hungry and urgent as his lips plundered hers. She found that far more telling than all the denials he might have uttered about his feelings for her.

"Damn," he murmured eventually, still holding her against him and looking more bemused and upset than ever. "You must have bewitched me or something."

Dani felt a smile tugging at her lips. "Why would you say that?"

"Because I'm extraordinarily tempted to do something I vowed to myself I wouldn't do again."

"Which is?"

"Make love to you."

Puzzled by the admission, she stared into his eyes. "Why would you have vowed never to make love to me again?"

"Because sooner or later, you're bound to get hurt."

"Why? I'm a grown-up. I know what I'm getting into here."

"Do you?" For a moment he avoided her gaze. When he finally looked into her eyes again, his expression was bleak. "It can't be any more than an affair, Dani,'' he said. ''And I know how badly you want marriage. Hell, you deserve marriage. Nobody deserves it more.''

Her heart seemed to go perfectly still. Panic made her almost breathless. ''Are you ruling out that possibility forever? Is this your final answer?''

His expression filled with sorrow, Slade nodded. ''I won't marry again, Dani. I'm no good at it.''

Astonished by his adamance even though he'd hinted at it before, Dani pushed aside her own fears and demanded, ''Where on earth did you ever get a ridiculous idea like that?''

''I was married before, remember? It wasn't exactly the most positive experience of my life,'' he said bitterly.

''Tell me about it,'' she pleaded. ''Don't I at least deserve to know about the one thing that seems to be standing between us?''

''You do, but I can't talk about it. If I'd understood what I was doing wrong with Amanda, I would have changed, or at least I like to think I would have. Now it's over and done with. We all paid a very high price for my first mistake,'' he said fiercely. ''I can't risk a second one.''

''What does that mean?''

''Bottom line? It means I'm sorry. It means I need to get out of here before I do something we'll both regret.''

Casting one last regretful look in her direction, he slammed open the screen door and walked outside.

Dani followed him, fighting tears and a terrible sense of desolation.

When he was halfway to his car, she called out.

He paused, but didn't look back.

"I could never regret anything that happened between us," she said. "Never."

She was almost certain she saw a shudder sweep over him at her words, but he climbed into his car and drove off anyway, leaving her feeling more alone than she ever had in her life.

Chapter Twelve

Naturally, since he'd declared to Dani that she was totally off-limits, he couldn't stop thinking of how desperately he wanted her. Perhaps she had known then what he had not...that he would never be able to resist her for long.

Two interminable weeks passed while he tried to stick to his promise to himself to avoid her. He was reduced to pleading with his sons to fill him in on what she was doing, how she looked, whether she'd asked about him. All in all, it was a very unsatisfying way to get information. He was frustrated as hell in more ways than one.

Maybe he was being ridiculous. Maybe she really knew what she was saying when she told him that she didn't expect marriage until and unless he wanted it. Maybe she could live with an affair, at least for the foreseeable future.

He tried very hard to convince himself that she was telling the truth, because believing her suited his purposes. His conscience, however, told a very different tale. And late at night he wondered if he wasn't stubbornly clinging to the past to protect his ego. No risk, no damage. How pathetic was that?

One morning after the third week without so much as a glimpse of her, he told his conscience to take a hike. Dani Wilde had gotten under his skin and there seemed to be nothing he could do to change that. He decided he might as well take her at her word and play this whole relationship out to see where it led. Once in a while he even dared to admit that he was falling in love with her.

Still, they needed time to be together, time to get to know each other that didn't involve two rambunctious, demanding little boys. Time to discover if she really wanted him...or just his sons. He needed to know for sure that he came first before taking a chance with his own feelings.

Accomplishing time alone required quite a bit of determination and ingenuity.

He'd made only a few friends since moving to town, and there were even fewer people likely to baby-sit the Watkins terrors, as they were not-so-affectionately known. Sara and Jake Dawson were among those who might be willing.

Slade eyed the phone doubtfully, weighed the implications of asking the couple to do him this favor, then sucked in a deep breath and dialed. At least Trent was still out of town and wouldn't be drawing all sorts of conclusions from his request.

Sara answered. Slade wasn't sure if she was the one he would have chosen to explain his dilemma to, but she said Jake was away from the house.

"I was wondering," he began, then hesitated.

"Yes?"

"I know it would be a big imposition."

"What would?" She chuckled at his reticence. "Come on, Slade, spit it out."

"Could you and Jake keep an eye on the boys for me this evening?"

"Oh," she said sweetly. "Isn't Dani available?"

Her tone suggested that she knew perfectly well how he intended that Dani be occupied, but she was going to drag it out of him. In fact, she seemed to be getting a huge kick out of making him spell it out. Maybe this was the payback he deserved for putting her sister on hold for the past three weeks, while he wrestled with his conscience and his growing vulnerability to this amazing woman.

"Maybe this was a bad idea," he muttered.

"No, it's not," she said hurriedly. "Jake and I would be happy to watch the boys. You could bring them out here now and they could spend the rest of the day and the night."

"That's not necessary," he protested. "A few hours would be plenty."

"Not if you have in mind what I think you have in mind," she retorted.

"I beg your pardon?"

"Just bring the boys out here now, Slade. They'll be fine overnight."

"Pirate, too?" he asked skeptically. "They won't spend the night there without him. The blasted dog's a nuisance."

"We'd be happy to have him," Sara assured him. "It's a ranch. We love animals."

"Thanks, Sara. I can't tell you what this means to me."

"Oh, I can imagine," she said dryly. "But I'm doing it for Dani, not you."

Slade ignored the implications of that remark. "We'll be there in about an hour, if that's okay with you."

"See you then."

"Oh, one last thing, Sara."

"Yes?"

"You will let me be the one to tell Dani about my plans for tonight, won't you?" he inquired dryly.

She laughed at that. "Sure, but you'd better get in touch with her real quick. I'm very bad at keeping secrets, especially secrets this juicy."

"She'll be my next call," he promised.

Unfortunately, Dani wasn't answering her phone. She'd probably gone out to make a delivery to the general store. Slade was far too anxious to set his plan into motion to wait around for her to get back.

"Kevin, Timmy, get your pj's and toothbrushes. You're going out to stay at Three-Stars."

Both boys raced into the kitchen. "We are? How come?" Timmy asked.

"Because Sara and Jake invited you," he explained, stretching the truth. "And I thought you'd have a great time."

"Pirate, too?" Kevin asked as the dog stared up at Slade hopefully.

"Yes, Pirate, too."

Timmy's gaze narrowed suspiciously. "What about you? Where will you be?"

"I have a few things to take care of."

"Like what?"

Slade tried to rein in his exasperation. "Timmy, don't you want to go to the ranch?"

His son's chin set stubbornly. "Not without you."

"I do," Kevin said. "Let Timmy stay here."

"You're both going. I have some things to do, and Sara and Jake volunteered to look after you."

"How come we can't stay with Dani?" Timmy asked, his expression mutinous.

"Because she's busy."

"Dani's never too busy for us," Timmy protested. "I'll bet if I ask her, we can stay with her." He started to reach for the phone.

"No," Slade said more harshly than he'd intended. Timmy's eyes filled with tears. "I'm sorry. I didn't mean to yell. Please, son, just take my word for it. Dani cannot baby-sit you tonight."

"I'm not a baby, anyway," Timmy declared. "I'm almost eleven. I can stay by myself."

"You cannot."

"Then let me come with you."

Slade was beginning to see every bit of progress the boys had made under Dani's care slip away. Timmy was reverting to the same difficult child he'd been when they'd first arrived in Riverton. He recalled the conversation they'd had a few weeks earlier and concluded that perhaps Timmy was worried that if Slade left them alone, they would never see him again.

"Timmy, there is no reason to be scared. It's only for one night," he assured him, hunkering down and looking his son in the eyes. "I will see you first thing tomorrow morning. I promise."

"I'm not scared," Timmy insisted. "I just don't want to go."

Now Kevin's chin started to wobble. "Does that mean we can't go? I want to." Huge tears rolled down his cheeks. "I love the ranch and the horses and everything."

Slade wondered how any single parent in his position ever managed to date again. He gathered both boys close and rested his chin atop Kevin's head.

"Guys, please, do this for me. It's really, really important or I wouldn't be asking."

Apparently well aware that the matter rested in his big brother's hands, Kevin turned his tear-streaked face to Timmy. "Please. Pirate and I will be with you every second. Nothing bad will happen."

Timmy, though, clearly understood what Kevin

did not, that bad things did happen all the time and that they often weren't within anyone's control. He shuddered, but then his expression turned stoic.

"Okay, do what you want," he muttered. "You will anyway."

Slade hugged him, grateful even for such grudging agreement. "Thank you."

He just prayed that he wasn't being totally selfish and giving Sara and Jake more trouble than the two of them could handle. Of course, Sara was a Wilde. She could probably handle an invading army without batting an eye.

It was almost 11:00 a.m. and there was no sign of Timmy and Kevin. Dani had gotten no answer when she'd tried to call Slade's house, either. What on earth had happened to them? They were usually here by eight, nine at the latest on those days when Slade got to working on the computer and forgot all about waking them.

She went over and over everything that had happened recently. Even though Slade had declared that he would not marry her or continue an affair with her, the boys had continued to show up at the house like clockwork. Only Slade had kept out of sight. It had been three weeks, one day and sixteen hours since she'd last set eyes on him.

Now the boys were missing, too. Was Slade worried that they were becoming too dependent on her? Had Timmy been asking about marriage again? Was Slade the kind of man who'd simply pack up his two kids and bolt because of the pressure she had put on him? She simply couldn't believe that of him. Besides, after his last and supposedly final declaration, she had forced herself to let the matter of marriage drop.

When the phone rang, she snatched it up on the first ring. "Yes?"

"My, my, you sound anxious," Ashley observed.

"Oh, it's you."

"Don't sound so thrilled. I thought you'd be in a better mood, all things considered."

"What things?"

Ashley fell silent.

"Ashley, what things?" Dani demanded.

"Never mind. I shouldn't have called. Bye."

She hung up before Dani could ask another single thing. She dialed her sister at home, but either Ashley had called from somewhere else or she wasn't about to pick up and answer questions.

Thoroughly unsettled, Dani called Sara, not really expecting to find her at home, either. She was usually off rounding up cows or something. To her surprise, though, Sara answered.

"Hi, what's up?" Sara said cheerfully.

"You tell me."

"What?"

"Oh, never mind," she said. Clearly Sara was going to be just as tight-lipped as Ashley.

"Dani, is everything okay?"

"Slade hasn't been by with the boys," she finally admitted. "He's not at home, either."

"I see." Sara drew in a deep breath. "Actually, the boys are here," she confessed, sounding ever so slightly guilty.

Dani was shocked. "At the ranch? Why?"

"They came for a visit, that's all."

"Sara, what is it you're not telling me?"

"Whoops, gotta run. Jake's calling. We're taking the boys on a picnic."

"Sara Wilde Dawson, don't you dare hang up on me."

"Bye-bye," her sister said, and then defied her by hanging up in her ear.

She glanced up from the phone to see Slade standing at the kitchen door. Somehow she knew that he was at the center of this sudden conspiracy of silence. Though she had to admit she was ridiculously glad to see him, her irritation with all the secrecy was stronger. She grabbed up a cast-iron skillet and waved it at him.

"Would you mind telling me what the hell is going on?" she demanded.

Slade grinned. "Uh-oh, somebody's got their drawers in a knot."

"Don't you patronize me, you rat. Why are the boys at Three-Stars? Why aren't they right here with me? And what do Sara and Ashley know that I don't?"

He held up his fingers and ticked off his answers. "One, I took them to Three-Stars. Two, because I want them there. And, three, they know that I have plans for you."

She stared at him. "Plans?"

He nodded. "Interested?"

"That depends."

"On?"

"Exactly what you have in mind." Though her annoyance was rapidly fading, it wasn't quite gone yet. He couldn't just come waltzing in here as if the past three weeks of separation had never occurred. He was going to pay for the misery he'd put her through.

She gave him a haughty look. "Why was I the last one to find out anything about these plans of yours?"

"Because you weren't here when I called earlier," he responded reasonably. "Where were you?"

"I took some things over to the store. I do have an answering machine, though. You could have left a message."

"And spoil the surprise?"

"Didn't you realize I'd worry?"

He had the grace to look a little guilty at that. "I suppose I should have thought of that. I was just anxious to take the boys to the ranch before Sara changed her mind about keeping them." He tried that winning smile on her again. "I got here as fast as I could."

Despite her exasperation, she was melting fast, no doubt about it. "Did you really?"

"I sped all the way. It was a wonder the sheriff didn't pick me up and lock me away."

"That fast, huh?"

He nodded and took a cautious step inside, one eye on the frying pan still in her hand. "Okay?" he asked. "Are you going to put that thing down or use it on my head?"

She set the skillet carefully on the stove, then tilted her head to study him. "You look awfully smug about something. What's on your mind?"

"Sex," he said.

He looked so darned serious that she had to smother a laugh. She was beginning to get the picture. No wonder he'd been racing around the countryside this morning. If she was reading his eagerness correctly, she found it rather touching. No, she corrected, it was actually downright thrilling. No need to let him know that, though. Clearly he'd thought things through and changed his mind about the two of them. She wondered why.

"Oh, really?" she commented, fascinated. "And how did that notion get planted in your mind when you went to great lengths to tell me we could never have sex again?"

"You put it there."

Her mouth dropped open at that. "I haven't even seen you."

"Precisely."

Her pulse skipped. This was very encouraging. "Did you miss me?"

"That's one explanation," he agreed. "At any rate, I've been thinking."

"About me," she concluded.

"About you," he confirmed.

"So you dumped the kids on my sister and came over here for sex?"

He blinked at the blunt summation. "It wasn't that way," he protested. "At least, not exactly."

Dani found she was rather enjoying this. The collapse of his resistance was definitely worth the agonizing wait. "Do you or do you not want to have sex with me?"

A spark of pure desire flared in his eyes. "Oh, yes," he said softly, catching her in his arms. "But not until after I've wined you and dined you."

"At eleven-thirty in the morning? We'd have to go to Stella's Diner, and that's awfully public for what you apparently have in mind."

"Forget Stella's, definitely. We could start with a picnic," he suggested. "And take it from there."

Now that he'd apparently overcome all those doubts and qualms he'd been spewing on his last visit, Dani wasn't taking any chances that a delay would get him to thinking again. She framed his face with her hands and looked directly into his eyes. "I say we start with breakfast in bed."

His lips curved into a smile. "Do you, now?"

"Any objections?"

"Not a one."

She stood on tiptoe and pressed a kiss against his mouth. "Breakfast won't take but a minute to fix."

"A minute's far too long to wait," he said, and claimed her lips again with a hungry, demanding kiss that set off a swarm of butterflies in her tummy and sent all thoughts of breakfast scattering.

"It is, isn't it?" she murmured, and headed for the stairs, Slade in tow.

She had reached the bedroom door when a thought struck her. "Damn," she murmured.

She looked up to find Slade's worried gaze fixed on her.

"What's wrong?"

"Nothing, I suppose."

"Dani, if you want to wait, it's okay. This isn't the way I'd planned for this to happen, anyway."

"No, no," she assured him. "It's not that. It's just that…" She hesitated. How could she tell him that the next time they slept together, she'd wanted to be wearing slinky black lace lingerie that would knock his socks off?

"What?" he prodded.

She gazed into his eyes, which had darkened with passion, and concluded that the kind of lingerie she wore didn't matter a hoot. Slade Watkins wanted her and he'd gone to great extremes today to have her.

If she had her way and if she was reading today's change of heart correctly, the black lace would do very nicely when they finally got around to a honeymoon.

Chapter Thirteen

Dani had absolutely no idea what had drawn Slade back into her arms after his firm declaration to stay away, but she wasn't about to fight it. The day they shared was thoroughly romantic and filled with so much passion that every minute she was sure he was only a breath or two away from making that lifelong commitment that so terrified him.

She fought the desire to nudge him just a little, convinced that she had already done all she could to prove that they were compatible in every respect. The decision about marriage was in his hands now. He had to wrestle with whatever demons there were from his first marriage and conquer them.

She sighed and opened her eyes to find him staring at her.

"I never knew that being with a woman could be like this," he told her, running his hand over her body, which stirred instantly. His slightest touch was proving to be pure magic. "You make me feel..."

She ended his search for the right word by suggesting lightly, "Exhausted?"

A smile tugged at the corners of his mouth. "I could never get tired of you."

Never, she thought happily. That was forever. An eternity. Why couldn't he get out the words that would guarantee that?

She reminded herself yet again to be patient. Everything was moving along quite nicely. Now was not the time to rock the boat. Besides, she had risked her pride once by asking him to marry her. She couldn't do it again.

"Shall we go out to dinner?" he asked, tucking a strand of typically wayward hair behind her ear. "I made reservations at the inn just outside of town. Everyone says they have the best food around."

Dani lifted an eyebrow. "Oh, really?"

He grinned at her testiness. "Outside of yours, of course."

"Smart answer."

"Shall we go and try some of their inferior food for dinner anyway?"

"We still haven't had breakfast," she reminded him, not bothering to hide her reluctance to leave what suddenly seemed to be a most enchanted home. As long as they remained safe, here in her bed, she was convinced nothing could tear them apart. "I promised you that hours ago."

"All the more reason to rally and go somewhere for a quiet, romantic dinner."

"I could fix dinner," she countered, fighting to keep from sharing him with the outside world.

"I want your attention on me, not on all your pots and pans."

With her gaze locked with his, she deliberately traced a finger down the center of his chest as she reminded him, "There's no privacy in a restaurant."

He grinned at her tactic and snagged her roving hand. "That is the trade-off." Without looking away, he provocatively drew each finger deep into his mouth, then asked, "Just how fast can you cook?"

Even with her knees so weak they probably wouldn't hold her, she vowed, "I can have a rejuvenating steak on the table in twenty minutes."

"Baked potato?"

She weighed the possibilities. "If you'll scrub them and pop them into the microwave, though I must admit I am offended by that particular shortcut. The skins wind up all wrinkly."

He chuckled at that. "I'm surprised you even own a microwave."

She shrugged. "It was a gift from Daddy. He thought it would get me out of the kitchen."

"Poor deluded man."

"He's not nearly as wise as you are. You love my cooking."

"Usually," he agreed. "Right now I'm just interested in sustenance. I think I might even settle for a couple of peanut butter and jelly sandwiches."

"I can definitely do better than that, but I'd better get started," she said, grabbing a robe off the chair beside the bed. "I'd hate to see your amazing stamina weaken."

"Not a chance of that with you around," he said, promising to join her downstairs in a minute.

The comment sent Dani off to the kitchen feeling very feminine and very smug. To her surprise it was still daylight outside, though evening shadows were finally beginning to stretch over the yard. The scent of her roses was drifting in the open window...along with the sound of a dog whimpering and a child's voice trying to shush it.

Curious, she opened the back door and saw a denim-covered bottom trying to disappear behind her hedge. She was pretty sure she'd seen that backside before.

She walked out onto the porch. "Timmy?"

Timmy didn't reply, but Pirate bounded out of the bushes at the sound of her voice. Tail wagging, he eagerly brushed up against her, covering her robe with streaks of mud. She sighed heavily and patted his head anyway.

"Timmy, I know you're here. You might as well come out of there."

With an obvious show of reluctance, he crawled back into view. Wide blue woebegone eyes regarded her. "I'm sorry," he whispered.

"About?"

"I ran away from Three-Stars and Dad is going to kill me."

Dani fought the desire to sweep him into her arms for a comforting hug. She just nodded. "He may, at that. Why did you run away?"

The frantic words tumbled out in a rush. "Because I didn't want to be at the ranch. I wanted to be with you, but Dad said I couldn't and he wouldn't tell me where he was going or anything. I don't even know where he is or if he's ever coming back. I'm sorry if you're mad at me."

Dani let her instincts take over. She opened her arms and gathered him close. "Oh, sweetie, I could never be mad at you, not for long, anyway."

"But Dad is going to kill me, isn't he?"

Before Dani could reply, the very man in question appeared in the doorway. His expression reflected a mix of incredulity and fury. "Timothy Watkins, what are you doing here? And why is that blasted dog getting mud all over everything? Pirate, sit!"

Pirate obediently trotted to his side and sat, panting. Slade didn't appear mollified by the response. He was still scowling.

Timmy's eyes were wide as saucers. "Dad, you're here? Why didn't you tell me you were going to be here?"

"I'm the one asking the questions," Slade countered sternly. "I left you twenty miles away. What the devil are you doing here?"

He looked as if he might keep on going, getting

himself more riled up with every word, but Dani cut him off.

"I'm just getting the details," she said firmly enough to silence whatever explosion was on the tip of Slade's tongue. Apparently he realized that losing his temper wouldn't accomplish anything, because he just folded his arms across his chest and glared at his son. He didn't look especially pleased with her, either, Dani decided.

Timmy clung to Dani even more tightly. She loosened his hold and knelt to face him. "You're going to have to deal with what you've done. Jake and Sara are probably worried sick."

He darted a quick glance at his father before admitting, "They don't even know I'm gone. They went on a picnic hours and hours ago, but I stayed at the house with Annie. I told her I was going to watch TV in Jake's office, but as soon as she went back to the kitchen, I ran away."

Dani could just imagine how frantic the housekeeper would be by now. Chances were Jake and Sara were back and freaking out, as well. "Sweetie, you know what you did was wrong. You'll have upset Annie terribly. She'll blame herself for not watching you more closely."

Timmy's expression turned pleading. "But it's not her fault," he insisted.

"No, it's not, but you were her responsibility. Annie takes that kind of thing very seriously. Go and call her right this second. Push number one on the speed dial,'' Dani said, giving him a push toward the door. "I'll talk to your father."

Timmy darted a fearful look at his father's stony expression, then regarded Dani gratefully. "Would you?"

He seemed to think that she could get him off the hook. Judging from Slade's tight-lipped fury, Dani had her doubts about that. "Oh, you're not going to be out of the woods, I promise you, but I think maybe I can persuade your father not to kill you."

Timmy ran inside without waiting to find out how successful she was.

"You're going to have to talk awfully fast," Slade warned her. "What he did was wrong. He openly defied me."

Dani searched for some way to mediate, but this entire episode was beyond her frame of reference. Besides, Slade was right. Running away had been wrong. And dangerous.

"Okay, let's say for the sake of argument that you're right," she began.

"I am right!"

She scowled at him. "Isn't the real issue here Timmy's safety?"

"That's one of them," he agreed. "How the hell did he get here, anyway?"

"He didn't say, but he is here and he is safe. Pirate came with him."

"Oh, that's reassuring," Slade said sarcastically. "That dog would be about as much protection as a pet gerbil." He stared at her incredulously. "Didn't you even ask how they got here?"

"It wasn't the first thing out of my mouth, no. I just wanted to be sure your son was okay. I figured he had to be pretty desperate to pull a stunt like this."

Slade didn't appear to be appeased. "Desperate? What does a ten-year-old know about desperation?"

"Enough, if he's just lost his mother and thinks his father is about to disappear."

"I told him—"

"You told him you wanted him to stay at the ranch. You didn't explain anything about your plan to spend the day with me, did you?"

"No," he said irritably. "I figured that was none of his business."

"Maybe not the details," Dani agreed. "But he obviously needed to know you'd still be close by, that he could reach you if he needed to."

Slade scowled at her. "Who the hell are you to tell me how to raise my son?" he lashed out at her.

Dani reacted as if he'd slapped her. Hearing Timmy declare a few days earlier that she was not his mother had hurt, but this was worse. Timmy was a child, who had no notion that words could cut deeply. Slade was old enough to know the precise damage they could do. He had entrusted Timmy to her care because it was convenient apparently, not because he respected her or trusted her.

How could she have been so wrong? She had

been so sure that Slade thought of her as a partner of sorts, at least where his sons were concerned.

"I care about them, too," she reminded him, her voice barely above a whisper.

"That doesn't mean you get to jump in and defend them when they've done something wrong." His complexion turned ashen. "My God, Dani, he could have been killed getting here. He could have been hit by a car or kidnapped."

She shivered at the fury in his eyes. She recognized that much of his anger stemmed from horror at what might have happened. But since nothing had happened, it seemed to her there were more important issues to be addressed.

"Isn't why he felt the need to do something so drastic more important?" she asked quietly, trying to overcome his justifiable emotion with logic and reason.

"No," he insisted stubbornly. "It is not. Sometimes all that matters is that he learn there are certain things he absolutely, positively cannot do."

"What does that mean? Are you planning to beat the daylights out of him?"

He impatiently waved off the suggestion. "Of course not. I don't beat my kids, but they do learn there are consequences when they misbehave."

"Such as?"

"I may ground him for the rest of his life."

"Oh, that would be productive," she retorted.

"Well, I'm so sorry you don't approve, but the bottom line here is that these are my kids we're talking about and it's up to me to do whatever the hell it takes to protect them.''

"And I have no say in this?"

"No," he said with lethal calm. "You do not."

Dani simply stared at him. How could she have made such a dreadful mistake? How could she have gotten the crazy idea that she would ever be anything more to Slade and his sons than a glorified baby-sitter with no real authority at all? Heck, she wasn't even a paid baby-sitter, and she threw in sex as a bonus. How stupid did that make her?

She wrapped her arms around her middle, but that wasn't nearly enough to ward off the sudden chill that swept over her.

"I think you'd better get Timmy and go," she said, suddenly exhausted.

"Gladly," he snapped back.

"And I think perhaps it's time you made other arrangements for their care during the day," she added impulsively. "Obviously you don't trust my instincts where they're concerned."

He looked slightly guilty at that. "I never said—"

"Yes," she said firmly. "In so many words, that is exactly what you said. Now, I would appreciate it if you would just get the hell out of my house."

Slade appeared stunned by the display of temper, but he stalked off to get Timmy without another word. When he exited with the boy in tow, he seemed slightly calmer, but by now Dani was so furious herself that there was no room for any sort of rational conversation.

"Dani?" Timmy whispered, his face pale. "What's going on?"

Though his obvious dismay nearly broke her heart, she forced herself to remain impassive. "I'm sure your father will fill you in."

"But—"

"Come on, son. Dragging your heels is only postponing the inevitable."

The caution only seemed to make Timmy more determined to linger. "I don't want to go with you," he said, his chin tilted defiantly. "I want to stay here with Dani."

"Well, you can't, and that's final."

"I hate you," Timmy shouted.

Slade flinched, but said firmly, "Get in the car."

"Dani?" Timmy whispered plaintively.

There was nothing she could do. With tears stinging her eyes, she had to stand by and let them both leave—the boy and the man she loved. Watching Timmy's forlorn face staring at her as they drove away was heartbreaking. Dani tried to blink back the flow of tears, but in the end they rolled down her cheeks unchecked. She forced herself not to respond to Timmy until the car was out of sight.

"Goodbye, sweetie," she called after him softly.

Slade had never been so terrified and so furious in his entire life. Every time he considered what might have happened to Timmy when he wandered away from Three-Stars, panic turned his skin cold and clammy.

And Dani had defended the boy, mouthing a bunch of psychobabble about his motivations. Hell, Slade knew exactly what had sent Timmy off on that journey back into town. No one understood better than Slade the trauma Timmy had been through when Amanda died.

But that was beside the point. The point was Timmy could have gotten himself killed or kidnapped. There were plenty of nuts in the world today. That he had arrived at Dani's safe and sound was pure good fortune. He now knew that a neighbor of Jake's had spotted Timmy practically the minute he'd stepped onto the highway and had given him a lift right to Dani's door.

Why hadn't Dani been able to see that his fury grew out of love and concern? He wasn't an ogre. He didn't lack compassion. But she had looked at him as if he'd just torn the wings off a delicate butterfly, or something equally horrendous.

Well, it didn't matter now. He'd taken a stance and she had disagreed with him vehemently. She had had the audacity to accuse him of being unreasonable.

In the fast and furious flurry of words that had followed, he was sure he had said plenty that was unfair, but she was the one who'd booted the boys out permanently. Naturally, though, they blamed him for the fact that they wouldn't be spending any more time with her.

He winced when he thought of their dismay. Their shock when he had kept them home with him this morning had been visible. No explanation he could come up with had cut through their fierce disappointment. It was worse, in some ways, for Kevin because he had done nothing wrong. He felt betrayed by his father, his brother and Dani.

Maybe it had been a thoroughly impulsive decision on Dani's part, but now that she'd made it, he doubted she would back down. Not that he could blame her for that. Everything had gotten wildly out of hand the day before. He had been unintentionally cruel and insulting. He could see that now. No one loved those boys or took better care of them than she did. She loved them as if they were her own.

But even recognizing that, he couldn't back down, no matter how much Timmy pleaded and Kevin cried. He knew they missed Dani. Hell, he missed her, too. That didn't matter. All that mattered was protecting Kevin and Timmy from harm.

Sara and Jake had tried to intercede the night before when they'd dropped off Kevin, but Slade had told them he was handling the matter the best way he knew how. He could see from Sara's expression that she blamed herself for everything that had happened. He had told her she wasn't at fault, that no one could have foreseen Timmy's determination and resourcefulness, but he doubted he'd managed to put much sincerity into his voice. Timmy's little escapade had happened on her watch.

Slade wasn't sure exactly when he realized that the house was entirely too quiet. He had been assuming that both boys had retreated to their rooms to play games on their computers. He should have known that since they'd made new friends, the computers and isolation no longer held the same appeal.

He tapped on Timmy's door, then opened it. There was no sign of the boy.

Only mildly alarmed, he checked Kevin's room. When he found that empty as well, he thundered downstairs and systematically checked every room in the house. There was no way to avoid the obvious: now they had both run away.

It didn't take a genius to figure out where they'd gone, either. Slade sighed and grabbed his car keys.

All the way to Dani's he tried to formulate a way of handling this latest escapade without another debacle. He still hadn't come up with one when he reached her porch.

The back door was standing open and she was visible through the screen door. Sitting at the table, surrounded by bowls and eggshells and bags of sugar and flour, she was perfectly still. It was that uncharacteristic stillness that made him pause before knocking.

She looked thoroughly lost, as if nothing mattered to her anymore. Slade was all too familiar with that kind of depression. The fact that he was responsible for Dani's anguish filled him with guilt.

Then he remembered why he had driven over here in the first place. He'd come for Timmy and Kevin, and Dani was no doubt hiding them. With his temper revived over this latest interference, he knocked.

She glanced up, but there was no familiar welcoming smile to warm his heart. There wasn't even any evidence of yesterday's anger. There was just a terrible kind of emptiness in her eyes. His heart ached for her, but he pushed the reaction aside as a temporary weakness.

"What are you doing here?" she asked.

"I'm sure you can imagine."

"Slade, I don't have the strength to play games with you. If there's something on your mind, just say it. If you've come to apologize, I accept. Just go."

He stared at her incredulously. "Apologize? Me?"

There was a brief flash of fire in her eyes as they clashed with his. "Isn't that why you came?"

"No. I came to get the boys."

Confusion registered on her face. "The boys? Why?"

"Don't play games, Dani. You can't protect them forever."

"Who's playing games? They're not here, Slade. I haven't seen either of them since you dragged Timmy out of here."

Suddenly outright panic replaced all the anger and tension. He grabbed her shoulders. "Are you telling me the truth?"

Furious sparks flared in her eyes. "I have never lied to you, Slade, and I resent you thinking I would about anything as important as this."

"I was so sure..." he began, and let the words trail off. He sank down on a chair then and stared at her. "Where could they be? Where the hell could they be?"

Chapter Fourteen

Dani couldn't look away from Slade's frightened, devastated face. Every angry thought she'd had about him, every furious curse she'd muttered during a long and lonely night vanished at the sight of his anguish. All that mattered right now was finding Timmy and Kevin. The disappearance of the boys they both loved had, at least for this one terrible moment, united them.

Trying not to let his panic fuel her own fears and immobilize her, she reached for Slade's hand to offer comfort and, hopefully, to restore calm. She needed his strength, as well.

Instinctively, he gripped her hand so hard she was certain he would crush the bones. She ignored the pain and hung on to him for dear life.

"When did you last see them?" she asked quietly.

He stared at her bleakly. "Right after breakfast. When they realized they weren't coming here today, they threw a tantrum and bolted for their rooms. I thought they were still there, but when I checked a few minutes ago they were gone." He closed his eyes. "Damn, I should have known they were too quiet. That always means trouble."

When she realized that until Slade's arrival she had been so lost in her own thoughts that she didn't know the time, Dani glanced at the clock. Relief washed over her. "It's not even lunchtime yet. They can't have been gone long," she said, hoping to reassure him.

"Please, Dani," he protested. "You and I both know that a couple of hours is a lifetime when you can stir up trouble the way those two can."

"Okay, let's be logical," she said, though she was feeling anything but. She wanted to give in to panic as Slade already had.

She could see so clearly now what she hadn't the day before; she could visualize all the dangers that could befall an intrepid boy. Slade, a product of life in bigger cities than Riverton, had seen them at once, but she'd been focused entirely on the fact that Timmy was with them and safe. She hadn't allowed herself to look back at what might have been.

Nor had she considered the possibility that he might repeat the same act less than twenty-four hours later. Perhaps this was the terrible struggle parents waged constantly, forced into a good cop–bad cop scenario when it came to discipline.

"I'm sorry," she said, clearly surprising him.

"About what?"

"Yesterday. I didn't understand what you were trying to do, that you wanted Timmy to feel a healthy fear of the dangers he'd risked by running away. All I could see was that he was scared and hurting."

"Didn't you think I saw that, too?"

She shook her head. "To be honest, no. I thought you were just being a bullheaded disciplinarian. Maybe if I hadn't taken Timmy's side, if I'd backed you up, he wouldn't be missing again."

"Stop," Slade insisted. "This isn't your fault. I was with them. I should have known they'd take off the first chance they got. I should have bolted the damn doors."

Dani managed a weak grin. "And put boards over all the windows?" she teased, finding a sliver of humor amid the desperate fear that was crowding in more and more with each passing second.

Slade sighed heavily. "No, I suppose nothing I could have done would have stopped them from leaving if they were intent on running away. But where would they go, if not here?"

"Back to the ranch?" Dani suggested.

He shot her a wry look. "I doubt it. Kevin loves it, but Timmy clearly doesn't. That's what started this, remember? I don't think he'd take refuge there."

"Maybe he went to apologize to Annie and Sara and Jake for what happened yesterday. He certainly felt guilty about worrying them so."

Slade looked skeptical, but he said, "I suppose you could be right. I'll call."

"And I'll run down to check with the Hinsons and the Bleeckers," she offered. "They might be hiding out there with their friends."

But her trip up and down the block was wasted. None of the other children had seen either Timmy or Kevin all day. Though she hadn't exactly doubted the trustworthiness of their word, she had checked with their parents, too. They hadn't seen either boy. All volunteered to help search for them.

Slade was outside when she came back. "Any sign of them?" he called out.

"Nothing. They're not at the ranch?"

"No, but Sara said she and Jake would start looking. They're calling Ashley and Dillon to ask them to begin searching, as well."

"The other parents in the neighborhood are already deployed to check out nearby streets," she told him. "We're going to find them, Slade. I promise."

He looked straight into her eyes then and lingered, as if drawing strength from her gaze. At that moment, she felt closer to him than she ever had. As bleak as things were, she felt hope.

"Thank you," he said quickly.

"Don't thank me. We haven't found them yet."

"But you've forgiven me for the hard time I gave you yesterday, haven't you?"

"You were scared out of your wits. How can I blame you for that?"

"You do know that everything I said came out all wrong, that I didn't mean half of it?"

She regarded him wryly. "But the other half you did?"

He winced. "No. Damn, I can't get anything right."

She dared to touch his cheek. "It's okay. Your mind is on Timmy and Kevin, where it belongs. Let's just concentrate for now on finding them."

"I don't even know where to begin looking."

He sounded so spent and frustrated that her heart ached for him. "What about the park?" she suggested. "They liked going there. Timmy loved playing baseball and he was so proud that you were his coach."

Slade looked doubtful, but he nodded. "You check there." Then, his expression defeated, he added, "I think I'd better go to the bus station and the train station."

Dani stared at him. "You think they would actually leave town?"

Slade raked a hand through his hair. "To be honest, I don't know what the hell they'd do. I didn't even think to check to see if they'd broken in to their piggy banks to take money with them. It just seemed like the logical next step."

"But where would they go if they left here?"

"Home to Denver, maybe. Or to Texas to meet my folks," he speculated.

"Do they even know where in Texas your family is?" Dani asked.

"No," he said wearily.

Sensing that he had to do something concrete, Dani encouraged him to go to the bus and train stations, even though she had a feeling that the boys weren't likely to stray away from Riverton. Maybe it was conceit on her part, but she was certain that they would eventually turn up at her house. If the threat of not seeing her was what had made them defy Slade and run away, then surely they would commit the ultimate act of defiance by seeking her out.

Before she could head for the park, Dillon and Ashley screeched to a stop in front of her house.

"Any sign of them?" Ashley called out.

"No. I was just going to the park to look."

"We'll go there," Dillon offered. "You stick close to home in case they turn up here."

Dani wanted to argue. She wanted to be doing something, not just sitting at home all alone, worrying and waiting, counting the minutes until they got some sort of news. But Dillon and Ashley were right. This was where she belonged. She'd thought it herself only moments before their arrival.

One by one the neighbors checked in with their reports. None of them had discovered any trace of either boy. Sara and Jake called to say there was no sign of Timmy or Kevin on the highway between the ranch and town. They'd started checking some of the less traveled roads out of town.

By one-thirty Dani was giving in to a full-blown attack of panic. She jumped at every noise. She clutched the portable phone so tightly it left an impression on her hand. Her silent commands that it ring went unheeded for the most part. When it did ring, the news was bleak. It was as if Timmy and Kevin had simply vanished without a trace.

At five minutes after two she heard a whispered hiss from the hedge between her house and Myrtle Kellogg's. Going to investigate, she found her highly agitated neighbor beckoning to her.

"Mrs. Kellogg, what on earth?" Dani demanded as the woman tiptoed toward her own back door.

"Shush," the older woman said. "If they find out I've told on them, they'll be fit to be tied."

"Who?" Dani asked, then realized the question was absurd. Mrs. Kellogg had been protecting Timmy and Kevin, of course. Relief flooded through her, followed almost at once by fury that they had been so close and Mrs. Kellogg had done nothing to let her know that. One look at the older woman's worried expression, though, told her that she had done the only thing she thought she could. Dani followed her next door, praying that she'd guessed right, that she would find Timmy and Kevin there.

Sure enough, there they were, sound asleep on the floor in front of the TV, the familiar soap opera blaring away in front of them. Tears welled up in Dani's eyes at the sight of them.

"I came as soon as my show went on," Mrs. Kellogg explained. "They were so tuckered out, it put them right to sleep." She faced Dani indignantly. "Would you mind telling me what you and that father of theirs have been doing to upset them so?"

Dani was still trying to gather her thoughts. She couldn't believe the boys had been practically under their noses all along. "They've been here all day?"

"Since nine-thirty or so," her neighbor admitted. "They got hysterical every time I mentioned calling you or their father. I didn't know what to do."

"You're the adult," Dani said impatiently. "Couldn't you have insisted? Didn't you realize we were scouring the whole town for them?"

"Well, of course I did. Do you think I couldn't see all that commotion outside? But they said neither of you wanted them and begged to live with me. That is not the kind of thing I take lightly." She glowered at Dani. "Now, something isn't right here and I want to know what it is."

"They have it all wrong," Dani swore to her. "It's just a huge misunderstanding, I promise. Please, keep them with you while I go let Slade know they're okay."

Mrs. Kellogg blocked her path. "Not until you've explained."

"Just let me find Slade. I'll explain later. It's a long story."

Mrs. Kellogg's expression was intractable. "I'm listening now," she said. "Those boys wouldn't have come to me with such a tale unless something was terribly wrong."

Dani sighed and conceded defeat. Clearly, her neighbor wouldn't be satisfied until she knew the whole story. Dani opted for the short version.

"Slade and I disagreed over how to handle something that happened yesterday. We argued. I told him not to bring the boys back. When they found out, I guess they assumed I didn't want them and they were mad at their father for causing the rift in the first place."

"But this was just a misunderstanding?" Mrs. Kellogg demanded. "I've watched the lot of you all summer long. I could just tell that something special was brewing. Surely, you and that young man are not foolish enough to break up over a silly misunderstanding. That's the trouble with young people today. They just cut and run the minute things get too difficult for them."

"I don't want to run, but it's not entirely up to me," Dani said with regret.

Suddenly Mrs. Kellogg's attention shifted to the doorway behind Dani. "What about you, young man? Do you intend to put things to right?"

All of Slade's attention was focused on his sons. The relief that washed across his face was visible. "Thank God," he murmured. "They look worn out. Did someone find them and bring them back?"

Dani shook her head. "They've been here all along. They thought neither of us wanted them anymore, so they begged Mrs. Kellogg to take them in.''

Slade looked thunderstruck. ''How could they think that?''

''A few actions, a couple of offhand comments and very vivid imaginations,'' Dani suggested. ''We gave them all they needed to reach that conclusion.''

''And my relationship with their mother didn't help.'' He looked at Dani. ''I have to show them that things are different with us.''

Dani's heart filled with hope.

''And I want to know how you intend to fix things,'' Mrs. Kellogg said, looking from one to the other. She waved them toward her kitchen. ''In there, both of you.''

Slade started to protest, but she cut him off. ''They'll be just fine where they are. In the meantime, I want some answers. It's not right for these children to think they're unwanted.''

''Mrs. Kellogg, nothing could be further from the truth,'' Slade insisted. ''I would give my life for those two.''

''So would I,'' Dani said softly.

Slade's gaze caught hers. There was guilt reflected in the depths of his eyes. ''I'm sorry if you thought I didn't know that. You've been wonderful with them. Sometimes I've envied you the rapport you've built with them in such a short time.''

''They were easy to love,'' Dani said. She hesitated, drew in a deep breath, then added bravely, ''So were you.''

Mrs. Kellogg nodded in satisfaction, then turned to Slade. "Well, what do you have to say for yourself?"

Slade grinned in the face of her determination to smooth over troubled waters and ensure that the boys would awaken to find that Slade and Dani had put their differences behind them. Dani rather admired the older woman for not backing down. She hadn't realized just how strong the bond between her and the boys had grown.

"I'm waiting," Mrs. Kellogg said to Slade.

He turned to Dani. "Maybe we should discuss this in private."

Mrs. Kellogg looked so disappointed that Dani decided on the spot that anything Slade had to say should be said right in her neighbor's kitchen.

"I'm comfortable discussing it right here," she advised him, settling into a chair and earning a gratified look from their hostess.

Slade appeared thoroughly uncomfortable, but he finally nodded. "Have it your way, then." He sat down, then reached over and took Dani's hand in his. As their gazes locked, he said quietly, "I accept."

"Accept?" Mrs. Kellogg said, looking confused. "Accept what?"

But Dani knew. A sensation of pure joy burst deep inside her, but caution forced her to study Slade's face intently. "Are you sure?"

"No, I'm scared to death," he answered honestly. "But if you believe in us, that's good enough for me. It's the only way I can think of to prove that I truly do trust your judgment.''

''Oh, for heaven's sakes,'' Mrs. Kellogg snapped impatiently. ''Will you two speak plain English?''

''Slade has just agreed to marry me,'' Dani told her.

''He has?'' Her expression brightened. ''Well, I'll be. That's better than I'd hoped for. When?''

Slade laughed. ''Maybe you should set the date.''

''Judging from the goings-on around here the past few weeks, I'd say it ought to be a short engagement,'' the older woman declared. ''Perhaps a lovely fall wedding would be best.''

''But it's only the beginning of August,'' Dani said wistfully, before she could stop herself.

Both Slade and Mrs. Kellogg chuckled.

''There's nothing more satisfying to a man than an anxious bride,'' Mrs. Kellogg observed. She looked Slade up and down. ''Of course, he is quite a fine specimen. Cuter than that young man on my soap, who has all the women in a dither. And he's a cad, besides.'' She frowned at Slade. ''You're not, are you?''

''I hope not.''

''That's a start. You may have to work to put a little more conviction into your voice, though,'' she said with a smile.

''Then you approve of my choice?'' Dani asked her.

Mrs. Kellogg nodded. ''If there was another one like him at home, I might go after him myself.''

''Unfortunately for you, he's one of a kind,'' Dani told her. ''And he's mine.''

''You're a brave woman, Dani Wilde,'' Slade told her, drawing her into his lap.

She folded her arms around his neck. ''Why? Because I love you?''

''Because you're marrying me.''

A shocked gasp from the doorway had them all turning to find two sleepy boys staring at them, openmouthed.

''You and Dani are getting married?'' Timmy asked cautiously. ''For real?''

''For real,'' Slade said. ''If you approve.''

''Oh, wow!'' Kevin said, coming awake and barreling across the room to envelop Dani in a hug. ''Oh, wow! That's the best.''

''Timmy?'' Dani asked quietly, her heart in her throat. ''What do you think?''

He kept his gaze averted for so long that her spirits sank. Finally he looked at his father. ''You're not going to mess things up, are you?''

''Not if I can help it,'' Slade promised. ''This is forever.''

''Swear it,'' Timmy insisted.

Slade met his son's gaze evenly and solemnly lifted his hand to sketch a cross on his chest. ''Cross my heart.''

Timmy still seemed uncertain. He looked toward Mrs. Kellogg, who smiled encouragingly. ''All anyone can promise is to try their very best,'' she told him.

Timmy finally looked at Dani. "Is that good enough for you?"

Unable to speak, she simply nodded.

At last a grin broke across his face. "All right," he whooped, doing a high five with his brother. "We're gonna have a mom!"

Tears spilled down Dani's cheeks at his words. She looked over and met Slade's gaze, trying to determine if he was even half as thrilled as the boys. His expression was unreadable.

And yet he had said yes. Wasn't that all that really counted? If she tried hard enough, maybe she could make herself believe it was.

Chapter Fifteen

As the neighbors one by one discovered that the boys were safe, Myrtle Kellogg's backyard turned into a huge block party. People pooled soft drinks from home. Dani supplied cookies and pies. Ginny Hinson and Francis Bleecker made up mounds of sandwiches.

Not until Ashley and Sara were there, though, did Dani make her big announcement. For once, the boys didn't blab a word of the secret.

Observing her sisters with their husbands, for once she no longer felt that terrible pang of envy that she'd never been able to deny. Now she had her own marriage to look forward to, plus a ready-made family.

She gazed up at Slade. "Last chance to back

out," she advised him. "Once I tell my sisters, you're on the hook for sure. And they'll get word to Daddy somehow, which will really seal your fate."

To her relief, he didn't look especially daunted by the warning. He leaned down and kissed her. "Don't worry. I have no intentions of trying to wriggle off. Just this one day without you was pure hell."

"No more ghosts from the past?"

After a moment's hesitation, he shook his head. "From now on, I'm looking ahead."

"Okay, then, here goes," she said, and reached for a can of soda. She raised her voice and asked, "Does everyone here have something to drink? I'd like to propose a toast."

Everyone grew quiet at once. Ashley and Sara crossed the yard until they were right in front of her, speculative expressions on their faces as they looked from Dani to Slade and back again.

"First of all, Slade and I would like to thank all of you for helping us today," she said as he tucked her hand securely in his. "Your willingness to search for Timmy and Kevin and your support reminded us of what makes Riverton such a special place to live."

"Amen to that," Slade said. "I will never forget what you did." He glanced at the boys, his expression sobering. "Or what you did, young men. You're going to be grounded until you leave for college."

"Whoops," Timmy said.

"I told you Dad was going to kill us," Kevin said, looking hopefully toward Dani for salvation.

"If he doesn't, I may," she said. "But we'll deal with that later. Right now I have an announcement to make." She paused to let anticipation build, then grinned at the man beside her. "Slade and his boys have just agreed to become my family."

Applause and shouts of encouragement greeted the news. Ashley and Sara rushed forward to hug Dani and her fiancé.

"Was it the lingerie or the perfume that did it?" Ashley whispered.

Apparently Slade overheard her. "What lingerie?" he demanded.

"Never mind," Dani said tartly. "You'll see it soon enough."

Suddenly a knowing grin spread across Slade's face. "That was it, wasn't it? The day I couldn't figure out what the heck had changed about you?"

The man had the memory of an elephant and the tenacity of a damned bull. "We'll discuss it later," Dani repeated, a blush climbing up her neck.

"Oh, yes," he murmured. "We will definitely discuss it later. Maybe we'll even have show-and-tell."

Her pulse ricocheted wildly. "You wish. I'm thinking there will be no more showing or telling until the honeymoon."

He looked properly horrified by the idea. "In that case, let's move that wedding date up a month or so," he pleaded fervently.

She grinned. "I told you long engagements were a bore. How about Labor Day weekend? We could sneak in a three-day honeymoon before school starts."

Slade was clearly disappointed. "I was thinking about a three-week honeymoon, after school starts, when the boys are safely tucked away inside a classroom."

"And just who were you planning to leave them with?" she inquired.

He glanced hopefully toward Sara and Jake. "Oh, no," Sara protested when she realized what he was suggesting. "I've already lost track of one of them."

His gaze shifted thoughtfully toward Ashley and Dillon. Ashley grinned at her husband. "You could handle them. They're little angels compared to the way you were at their age."

Dillon regarded the boys in question skeptically. "I suppose we could tie them to a bedpost the minute they got home from school," he said seriously, then hauled them into his arms for a bear hug when they looked horrified by the suggestion. "Hey, we'd have a great time. I could teach you to drive my Harley."

Now it was Slade's turn to look horrified. "Maybe we'd better settle for that three-day honeymoon, after all. The boys can come, too."

"All right!" Kevin shouted. "We're going on a honeymoon." Then his expression sobered. "What's a honeymoon?"

"Never mind, squirt," Timmy said. "I'll explain it later."

Slade frowned at him. "Just leave out the part about sex, okay?"

"What's sex?" Kevin demanded.

"Never mind," Slade said adamantly. "We'll go for a week if you'll just keep your mouth shut."

"All right!" both boys chorused.

Ashley grinned at Dani. "I'm so relieved."

"About what?" Dani asked.

"You've had them all summer long and not even you have been able to tame them."

"And why is that such a relief?"

"I'd hate to think my good influence could eventually turn Dillon into an angel. Now I'm more convinced than ever that once they're a rebel, they'll always be a rebel."

Slade sighed heavily and tugged Dani close. "Somehow I don't find that nearly as reassuring as she does. I was hoping not to have gray hair before my thirty-fifth birthday."

Grinning, she reached up and plucked a strand of gray from amid the dark blond. "Too late, sweetie."

Dani's wedding day dawned bright and clear on the first Saturday in September. She had won that particular battle. Ashley and Sara had pitched in with the arrangements to ensure that it would be the wedding of her dreams, despite the short notice.

All in all, everything was going smoothly. Kevin and Timmy were finally off the restrictions that

Slade had insisted on after their disappearance. He'd grounded them for two weeks, not the years he'd threatened. In fact, the boys had been little angels ever since they'd learned that Dani was about to become a permanent part of their lives. Dani seriously doubted the good behavior would last forever, but she'd been grateful for it with so many other things on her mind.

Now, though, despite the gorgeous weather, despite her incredible gown, which Ashley had wrangled straight from the designer's workroom, and despite a church filled with imported tropical blossoms all the way from Hawaii—the latter a prelude to their planned week-long honeymoon on Maui, alone thanks to her father's offer to baby-sit—there was a huge cloud of doubts hovering around her heart.

Even as she fiddled with her veil and listened to Sara and Ashley chattering and laughing about the success of their plan to seduce Slade Watkins into Dani's arms, she wondered what was missing. This should be the happiest day of her life, but there was a knot deep inside her that couldn't be attributed entirely to nerves.

She was about to marry a man she loved with all her heart. She would be mother to two boys she already adored beyond reason. Why was there this terrible cold, twisting sensation in the pit of her stomach?

Why? Why? Why? The word tormented her. Why was Slade marrying her? Just because she'd asked? Never. Just because of his sons? She doubted it. To legitimize sleeping with her? Probably not. Why, then?

Not once during all of these frantic days of preparations had he ever admitted he loved her, just that he was putting his past to rest. And love, of course, was the only thing that she really wanted.

Suddenly, with less than a half hour to go before the ceremony, she realized she had to know just how deeply he truly cared.

"Stop fussing," she instructed her sisters. "I'm as presentable as I'm going to be."

"You're more than presentable," Sara chided. "You're beautiful."

"And you're biased. Now, if you want to make yourselves useful, go find Slade and bring him back here."

"Right before the wedding?" Ashley asked, clearly scandalized by the request. "I don't think so. Everyone knows it's bad luck for the groom to see the bride right before the wedding."

Dani scowled at her. "I will not walk down the aisle until I've talked to him."

"Oh, God," Sara moaned. "I knew this was going to happen. Dani, you were always too sensible to go through with a scheme like this. What are we going to tell the guests?"

"Worse," Ashley said, "what are we going to tell Daddy? He's jumpy enough about all of this. He's furious he wasn't here to watch this love story unfold. Now he can't take credit for making it happen."

"Would you two just stop," Dani pleaded. "Don't say a word to Daddy. The less he knows about this, the better. Let Mrs. Fawcett keep him calm. He's going to need all of his wits about him if he's going to watch Timmy and Kevin for us while we're in Hawaii."

"I suspect Mrs. Fawcett would like to wring your neck herself for dragging them back here before they had their own wedding," Ashley noted, then grinned. "Of course, she does get a rather wicked glint in her eyes when she thinks about shaping Timmy and Kevin into model young citizens. Maybe that will pacify her."

"Or maybe she and Daddy can make use of the minister and the church, if Dani backs out," Sara suggested, her expression bleak as she considered the possibility of the whole day and all their hard work going up in smoke.

Dani rolled her eyes. "For goodness' sakes, stop fretting. I am not backing out of anything. There won't be anything to tell Daddy or the guests if you'll just get Slade in here so he and I can talk." She gazed at Ashley, who seemed to be in a more reasonable frame of mind. "Please?"

Five minutes later Slade was there, accompanied by both boys, their eyes wide with excitement. All three of them were dressed in tuxedos, though Timmy's and Kevin's were already rumpled, their bow ties slightly askew, their shirts untucked. Kevin's black pants had a suspicious streak of mud, suggesting that Pirate was somewhere in the vicinity, even though the dog had been banished for the day. Slade apparently wasn't yet aware of the interloper, since the boys were still in one piece.

"Dani, you look like a princess," Kevin asserted.

"You're beautiful," Timmy agreed. "The most beautiful bride ever."

Dani's heart warmed. They were her guys, all right. There wasn't a doubt in her mind about their love. It was their father who concerned her.

"Thanks, you two. I love you." She leaned down to kiss them both. "Now, could you do me a huge favor and go with Sara for a minute? I need to speak with your father."

Timmy apparently caught some undertone in her voice and promptly looked worried. "Is everything okay?"

"Everything is just fine," she promised, praying that she wasn't lying about something so important. He would be crushed if she and Slade let him down now.

"Run along," she prompted. "We'll be walking down the aisle in no time."

"And keep that blasted dog out of the church," Slade told them, proving that he was far more aware of things than Dani had guessed.

When they'd gone, Dani reached up and stopped Slade's fingers from fiddling with his tie. Clearly startled by her touch, he paused and gazed into her eyes. His expression instantly clouded with concern that mirrored his son's.

"Timmy was right, wasn't he? Something is

wrong. You're not about to back out on me, are you?''

She rested her hand against his cheek. Even so slight a contact reassured her. She absolutely tingled inside, proving once more that Slade was the only man for her.

"I'm not," she assured him. "How about you, though? Are you sure about this, Slade?''

There was no mistaking the slight hesitation before he managed to say yes. That infinitesimal pause scared the living daylights out of her. How could she go through with this if he had any uncertainties at all? How could he go through with it?

Worse, why the devil had she waited until they had a church filled with people before she forced a discussion of this? That one was easy, of course. She'd been terrified he would give her the wrong answer. She still was, but she wasn't the kind of woman who could back down from discovering hard truths.

"That wasn't very convincing," she told him as lightly as she could manage with fear clogging her throat. "Are you really sure this is what you want? Or have the boys and I badgered you into it?''

He took her hands in his and brushed a kiss across her knuckles. "Yes, this is what I want," he insisted a little more forcefully.

There was more conviction in his voice this time, but that earlier hesitation wasn't so easily overcome. "Why?'' she asked. "Because you want me?''

His answering grin was enough to make her pulse race. "That's definitely one reason."

But was it enough? she wondered. Passion was a good start, but for a marriage to last a lifetime, there had to be more. "Anything else?" she asked.

"Like Kevin said, you look like a princess."

She sighed. This wasn't going at all the way she'd hoped it would. "And?" she prodded.

There was an amused glint in his eye as he added, "To quote Timmy, you cook pretty good."

Oh, dear heaven, it was exactly as she'd feared. He was doing this for all the wrong reasons, she concluded with a sinking sensation of dismay.

"You could sleep with any one of the women in town who've been salivating over your body ever since you arrived," she pointed out.

"I didn't want them."

He seemed certain enough about that. That was good, but it wasn't enough. "I'm not a princess, Slade. I'm just a woman who wants a husband and family."

His obvious amusement faded as he realized how serious she was. "Me, I hope. And my family."

"You could hire a housekeeper. That might be less complicated."

"I like your cooking just fine. And my boys adore you." He stepped closer then and cupped her face in his hands. "It's you I want, Dani Wilde. Just you."

She couldn't seem to stop herself from asking one

more time, "Why?" It came out as a tremulous whisper.

"Because nobody could love me the way you do," he said at once. He brushed aside her veil and kissed her gently. "And there's nobody on earth I could love the way I love you."

She searched his face. "You're sure?"

"Absolutely. You amaze me, Dani Wilde. You amaze me with how much love you have to give, with your generosity, with your spirit, with your ability to cope with those two outrageous boys of mine. Destiny brought you into my life. You never gave up on me, on us. Now that we're together, I will never let you go. And I swear that I will do everything in my power to make you happy."

A sigh of relief whispered through her, followed by a bursting of pure joy. Dani felt as if she'd been granted God's greatest gift. "You already have." She paused. "There is just one thing—"

He cut her off. "I know."

She regarded him guiltily. "Know what?"

"I know that you slipped my parents into town for the wedding."

Dani winced. "You saw them?"

"How could I miss them? They're sitting in the first row of the church."

"Are you furious?"

"No, I love you all the more for caring enough to try to patch things up between us. Just be sure you're around to referee the first time we're in the same room together."

"Always," she agreed readily.

"Can we get on with this wedding now?"

Dani grinned at him. "You sound like a man in a hurry."

"I am. I can't wait to get a really good look at all that sexy lingerie you've been ordering by the truckload."

Slade actually spent very little time on their honeymoon admiring Dani's lingerie. In fact, he managed to get her out of it as quickly and as often as he could.

She never failed to startle and astonish him, he decided as he watched her sleeping so peacefully beside him, a smile on her lips.

Why had it taken him so long to realize what a treasure she was? How could he have had any doubts at all that having her in his life on a permanent basis was the smartest decision he would ever make?

He sighed with pleasure as she unconsciously reached for him, curving an arm over his belly as she slept. His body leapt to life at the innocent touch.

She was amazing, all right. But what amazed him most of all was that this one audacious imp of a woman had made a hardened old cynic like him believe in love and happily ever after.

Epilogue

Trent Wilde was exhausted, yet he gazed around the yard at Three-Stars and sighed contentedly. For an old man, he'd done pretty darned well, he concluded. He reached over and grasped the hand of the woman beside him.

"Well, Tillie, it looks as though my work here is just about done. All of my girls are happily married. Now maybe we can finally get around to that wedding we've been putting off."

Matilda Fawcett regarded him with blatant skepticism. "Trent Wilde, who do you think you're kidding? You've got a whole new generation to worry about now, what with Dani and Slade's boys giving everybody in town fits and Ashley's new baby on the way." She glanced at Sara. "Something tells me

Sara and Jake will be making an announcement of their own any minute now.''

Trent sat up a little straighter and gazed at his middle daughter. ''You think so? She hasn't said a word.''

''And why would she tell you first? You'd only pester her to death till the baby is born.'' She grinned at him. ''Maybe I should do her a favor and get you out of their hair.''

Trent kissed the hand he held. ''Are you finally saying yes, after all these years?''

Color crept into her cheeks. ''Well, I never thought I'd be marrying a younger man,'' she teased, ''but you haven't turned out so badly.''

''It took you long enough to see that,'' he chided.

''It always pays to use a little caution where you outrageous Wildes are concerned.''

''But forty years seems awfully long. Didn't you have the proof you needed long ago?''

''I did,'' she agreed. ''But by then you were happily married to someone else and so was I.''

''Now, at long last, it's our turn,'' he said, then grinned as a wicked scheme occurred to him. ''How do you feel about hopping on Dillon's Harley and eloping right this second?''

Her eyes lit up at the suggestion. Suddenly she looked like a young girl again, the woman he'd fallen a little bit in love with the first time she'd stepped into a classroom and tried to teach algebra to a class filled with troublemakers like him.

She laced her fingers through his. ''Why, Trent

Wilde, I do believe that's the best idea you've ever had."

He looked from her excited expression to the family that had brought him so much joy. "It's right up there with getting those girls of mine settled down, I guarantee you that. Come on, Tillie. Let's go walk down that bridal path while no one in this gang is the wiser."

"You sure you want to cheat them of the chance to be there?"

He looked across the lawn to where Ashley was leaning back in Dillon's arms, then moved on to Sara and Jake, who were side by side at the paddock fence, their hands linked as they laughed at the new foal just testing his legs.

And finally he turned to Dani, his firstborn, the one so much like his late wife she'd sometimes made his heart ache just looking at her sweet face. She and Slade were arguing over the placement of the swing set Trent had just bought for all the grandbabies he was anticipating. Timmy and Kevin were chiming in with their opinions as well, and that fool dog of theirs was running in circles, chasing his own tail and barking to beat the band.

Well satisfied with what he saw, he turned back to Tillie. "I doubt they'll even miss us," he told her. "Let's go get hitched."

They slipped silently away. They'd made it as far as Dillon's motorcycle when Trent heard Ashley's voice.

"Hey, Daddy, don't forget to buy her the biggest bouquet the florist has," she called out, laughing.

Trent scowled as the rest of them gathered around. "Never could put a darn thing over on any of you, could I?" he muttered.

"Try to remember that," Dani told him.

"Bless you, Daddy," Sara whispered in his ear. "Be happy."

"How could I not be," he said, his voice choked. "I'm about to add one more to the best family God ever gave a man."

* * * * *

RISING TIDES

the compelling sequel to *Iron Lace*

Aurore Gerritsen, matriarch of one of
Louisiana's most prominent families, has died.
And the future of her family is at stake.

Nine people—some family, others strangers, all
heirs to Aurore's fortune—have gathered for
four days for the reading of her will. As a lifetime
of family secrets are revealed one by one, those
present learn things that will irrevocably drive
some of them apart and bring others together.

bestselling author

EMILIE RICHARDS

Available in May 1997 at your favorite retail outlet.

MIRA The brightest star in women's fiction

As seen on TV!
Free Gift Offer

With a Free Gift proof-of-purchase from any Silhouette® book,
you can receive a beautiful cubic zirconia pendant.

This gorgeous marquise-shaped stone is a genuine cubic
zirconia—accented by an 18" gold tone necklace.

(Approximate retail value $19.95)

Send for yours today...

compliments of *Silhouette*®

To receive your free gift, a cubic zirconia pendant, send us one original proof-of-purchase, photocopies not accepted, from the back of any Silhouette Romance™, Silhouette Desire®, Silhouette Special Edition®, Silhouette Intimate Moments® or Silhouette Yours Truly™ title available in February, March and April at your favorite retail outlet, together with the Free Gift Certificate, plus a check or money order for $1.65 U.S./$2.15 CAN. (do not send cash) to cover postage and handling, payable to Silhouette Free Gift Offer. We will send you the specified gift. Allow 6 to 8 weeks for delivery. Offer good until April 30, 1997 or while quantities last. Offer valid in the U.S. and Canada only.

Free Gift Certificate

Name: _____

Address: _____

City: _____ State/Province: _____ Zip/Postal Code: _____

Mail this certificate, one proof-of-purchase and a check or money order for postage and handling to: SILHOUETTE FREE GIFT OFFER 1997. In the U.S.: 3010 Walden Avenue, P.O. Box 9077, Buffalo NY 14269-9077. In Canada: P.O. Box 613, Fort Erie, Ontario L2Z 5X3.

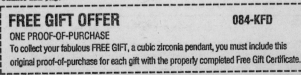

FREE GIFT OFFER   084-KFD

ONE PROOF-OF-PURCHASE

To collect your fabulous FREE GIFT, a cubic zirconia pendant, you must include this original proof-of-purchase for each gift with the properly completed Free Gift Certificate.

084-KFD

In April 1997
Bestselling Author

DALLAS SCHULZE

takes her Family Circle series to new heights with

TESSA'S CHILD

In April 1997 Dallas Schulze brings readers a
brand-new, longer, out-of-series title featuring the
characters from her popular Family Circle miniseries.

When rancher Keefe Walker found Tessa Wyndham he
knew that she needed a man's protection—she was
pregnant, alone and on the run from a heartless past.
Keefe was also hiding from a dark past...but in one
overwhelming moment he and Tessa forged a family
bond that could never be broken.

Available in April wherever books are sold.

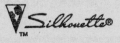